"I'm not hiring you to baby-sit.

"I want you for my wife," Thomas continued.

"Maybe you ought to spell out exactly what my duties as your wife would entail," Cheyenne said.

"This isn't about duty."

"All right. Function. Expectations. What would you expect from me?"

"You know, the usual." For the first time, a hint of discomfort crept into Thomas's manner.

"The usual. Ironing your shirts? Fixing meat loaf?"

"You're being deliberately obtuse."

"You're being deliberately vague. You want me to take care of your nephew and you expect 'the usual.' Would you sign a contract that used such ambiguous terms?"

"All right," he ground out. "I would expect to sleep with you."

Dear Reader,

Sitting in my red-wallpapered office, I'm surrounded by family photographs. I love seeing my husband as a baby, my father as an adolescent and my daughter at age four holding her new baby brother.

For better or worse, we all have families. I didn't plan to write about the Lassiter family, but as Cheyenne Lassiter formed in my mind I realized I was dealing with more than one woman, and her sisters, Allie and Greeley, came into being. Then their older brother demanded his story be told, and who can say no to a sexy man like Worth Lassiter? What started as one book had suddenly become four.

I hope you enjoy reading about the Lassiter family and the strong men—and woman!—who match them.

Love

Jeanne Allan

HOPE VALLEY BRIDES

Four weddings, one Colorado family

One Bride Delivered
Jeanne Allan

HOPE VALLEY BRIDES

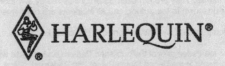

TORONTO • NEW YORK • LONDON
AMSTERDAM • PARIS • SYDNEY • HAMBURG
STOCKHOLM • ATHENS • TOKYO • MILAN • MADRID
PRAGUE • WARSAW • BUDAPEST • AUCKLAND

ISBN 0-373-03568-3

ONE BRIDE DELIVERED

First North American Publication 1999.

Visit us at www.romance.net

Printed in U.S.A.

CHAPTER ONE

Need wife to take kare of a little kid. Has to bake cookys, read storys and smile a lot. No hitting. Room 301, the St. Christopher Hotel, Aspen, Colorado.

THE advertisement leaped out at Cheyenne Lassiter as she sat at the breakfast table, and her spoon clattered down. Grabbing the newspaper with both hands, she reread the ad. The cantaloupe in her mouth lost all flavor. Cheyenne pushed the newspaper across the table to her younger sister. "Read this."

Allie scanned the ad. "A unique way to meet women."

"You think that's what it is?" Cheyenne hesitated. "It doesn't read to you as if a child had written it?"

Allie read the ad again. "Maybe. You're worried about the 'no hitting' part, aren't you?"

"Yes." Cheyenne took back the paper. "I know you all think I see a child-abusing parent on every corner, but..." Her voice died away.

"Michael is safe now," Allie reminded her. "Safe and happy living with his aunt and uncle."

"How could I have blindly ignored the way he'd never look me in the eye when he'd mumble he'd fallen down stairs or run into a door? But his mother volunteered in my classroom, and Mr. Karper showed such interest in his stepson's progress." Cheyenne stared at the ad with unseeing eyes. "I'll always wonder if I would have guessed the truth earlier if Michael had been poor and dirty."

"No one suspected Michael's stepdad knocked the poor kid around. Quit beating yourself over the head with it. The

5

minute you suspected what was going on, you went to the authorities. If it weren't for you, Michael might still be living with his mother and her husband. Or dead.''

"Michael must have despaired of being helped.'' Cheyenne rolled up the newspaper section. "I promised myself I'd never again shut my eyes to something right in front of me.'' Her gaze slid past her sister. "I don't meet the Brownings until ten.''

"Which means you think you have time to check out what's going on in Room 301 at St. Chris's.'' Allie tore a hunk from her bagel and handed it to the greyhound standing expectantly beside the table. "No one appointed you to save the world.''

"You're not supposed to feed the dogs at the table.'' Cheyenne pushed back her chair, carefully avoiding Allie's three-legged cat.

Allie tore off another hunk of bagel. "One of these days you're going to stick your nose into someone else's business and get it bit off.''

"All I'm doing is dropping by the hotel to say hi. If there's a problem, I'll notify the proper authorities. I have no intention of getting personally involved.''

"If I'm disturbed by one more female pounding on my door, I'm going to fire the entire staff.'' Thomas Steele slammed down the telephone receiver in the middle of the hotel manager's stammered apology.

The first woman had banged on the door of his hotel suite shortly after 6:00 a.m. Groggy with sleep, Thomas had snarled at her and the plastic bag of cookies he assumed she was selling. Before he could summon the manager for an explanation on exactly why solicitation was allowed to take place in a Steele-owned hotel, another woman had knocked on the door, followed by a procession of women, all shapes, sizes and ages, most bearing cookies, and all grinning like Cheshire cats.

Thomas rubbed a hand over his unshaven chin and considered the possibility that getting into his suite was part of a twisted game of scavenger hunt. McCall, the hotel's manager, claimed he knew nothing. One woman had garbled something about a newspaper. Thomas should have demanded an explanation before shutting the door in her face, but he wasn't at his best before coffee in the morning.

Slight stirrings came from an adjoining room. The boy was awake, but he wouldn't get out of bed until Thomas told him to. His nephew tiptoed around, obviously fearing the sky would fall if he even looked at his uncle. Thomas ran his fingers through his hair, knowing he'd brought this on himself. For a second, back in New York, he'd looked at the boy and seen someone else, and before he knew it, he heard himself saying he'd take the boy to Aspen. Now he was damned if he knew what to do with him. Thomas Steele, CEO of a chain of exclusive hotels, buffaloed by a six-year-old boy.

Picking up the phone, he ordered their breakfasts. He wasn't sure the boy actually liked oatmeal. When asked, the boy had shrugged, but oatmeal was the only breakfast food he'd eaten. Thomas made a mental note of the need for more child-friendly items on the menu.

Knuckles beat a tattoo on the suite's door bringing a mocking smile to his face. Breakfast had arrived in record time. People jumped when the boss was annoyed. He snugged the belt to his bathrobe and jerked open the door.

By the time Thomas realized the tall blond female standing in the hallway held no breakfast tray, she'd barged into the suite. About to escort her bodily back into the hall, he reconsidered. The time had come to stop this nonsense. When he finished with this woman, he'd make damned sure no one else disturbed him. Thomas slammed the door behind him and glared menacingly at her. No one could do menace the way he could.

The woman glared back.

At least she wasn't grinning like an ape. He glanced at her hands. No cookies. Just a rolled-up newspaper she batted in irritation against a bare leg. He didn't know why the hell she was irritated. He was the one being harassed.

Thomas allowed the silence to grow while he inspected his unwelcome visitor with insulting thoroughness. Lightly tanned legs extended forever below the bottom of ghastly khaki cuffed shorts before finally disappearing into thick white socks above sturdy walking shoes. Slowly he worked his gaze up past trim hips and a narrow waist.

And firm breasts. Undoubtedly held in check by a practical sports bra. Skin tanned to the exact shade of her legs showed in the open vee of her blue denim shirt. Thomas visualized white knit snugly cradling mounds of tanned flesh. A dull flush crawled up her neck. Apparently his visitor read minds. Giving a tiny smile of satisfaction, Thomas brought a heavy-lidded gaze to rest on her face.

Some men might consider her a beauty. If they liked tall, athletic, healthy-looking blondes. Thomas's taste ran to sleek, exotic, dark-haired women who oozed sophistication and sex. This woman oozed indignation. Thomas raised a mocking eyebrow, a gesture he'd practiced as a teen which now came naturally to him. He'd reduced more than one errant employee to gibbering justification and contrition with that eyebrow. Her bottom lip was too full to actually thin with annoyance, but the woman did her level best.

"No cookies?" he asked smoothly. She looked perplexed for a split second before awareness deepened her gray eyes—no, not gray, but light blue with a grayish-brown rim around the pupils.

"I assume that means you know all about it."

Thomas had seen the woman before. In passing on Aspen's pedestrian mall or— Of course. She must be an employee of the hotel. As of this second, close to being a former employee. "I know," he said in answer to her implied question, "you're dangerously close to never working for a Steele hotel again."

She gave him a startled look.

He let her think about his threat while he answered the knock on the door. The room service waiter smiled at the woman. Every person who worked at the St. Christopher Hotel would know to the second how long she'd been in Thomas's suite. They'd think he'd gotten soft. They'd be wrong. Once he found out what was going on, he'd deliver a tongue-lashing this particular interloper would never forget.

The door closed behind the waiter. The smell of coffee drew Thomas to the table, and pouring himself a cup, he drank deeply. The liquid scalded his mouth, but the caffeine jolted his brain into full power. Giving the woman a dark look over the rim of the cup, he sipped more deliberately.

The woman looked at the tray. "Breakfast for two."

Warning bells clanged in Thomas's head. As an extremely eligible bachelor, he knew the lengths to which marriage-minded women would go. Immediately he armored himself with a fictitious female companion. "Did you think I'd allow her to leave before she had breakfast?"

"I should hope not. She needs a good breakfast to start the day off right." The woman inspected the tray. "Milk, oatmeal. I don't see any fruit or juice. For proper nutrition, she needs two to four servings of fruit a day. Plus vegetables."

She was nuts. "I don't give a damn about her nutrition. All I care about is a certain level of performance. How she achieves it is her problem."

"You're her father. You ought to care."

"Father," he said blankly. "I'm talking about the woman in my bed."

"You have a wife?"

Her stunned surprise confirmed his suspicion she'd come

husband-hunting. "I'm unmarried and intend to stay that way."

"You don't have a wife, but you do have a woman in your bed," she said slowly. "And you can stand there and brag that all you care about is how good she is in bed? What kind of example is that for a child?"

"That's it. I've run out of patience. Tell me what the hell is going on."

Instead of answering, the woman moved quickly to his bedroom, knocked once, waited a couple of seconds, then opened the door. Next she'd be checking his pillow for stray hairs. Not that she'd find any. The boy had definitely cramped Thomas's social life.

After a quick survey of the empty room she headed for the boy's room and knocked again. In answer to a muted response, the woman opened the door and peered in. "Hi," she said. "Sorry. I didn't mean to bother you." Closing the door, she turned. "There's no woman here. Just your son."

Thomas shrugged, not bothering to correct her. "Maybe she went out the window."

"In broad daylight?"

"Stranger things than that happen in Aspen."

"Not nearly as strange as you trying to convince me you have a woman in your bed. I've heard of men bragging of their sexual prowess, but you take the cake, buddy."

"As you are well aware, my name is Thomas Steele." When she didn't react, he added smoothly, "One of the hotel Steeles."

"I suppose because your family owns this hotel you're rich and you do have a woman in your bed every night. Last night's candidate come down with the flu? Or a case of good taste?"

Thomas slammed his cup on the table. "Look, lady—"

"My name is Cheyenne Lassiter. One of the ranching

Lassiters.'' She mocked his earlier self-introduction. "And I'm the 'C' in C & A Enterprises."

For two cents he'd toss the impudent Ms. Cheyenne Lassiter out in the hall on her delectable bottom. Better yet, he'd toss her down on the carpet and turn the scorn in those muddy blue eyes to something else entirely. Hell, his brain had gone haywire. Served him right for trying to deal logically with a bunch of nutty women. "I have no idea why you and your friends are harassing me, Ms. Lassiter, but it stops now." Thomas sat at the dining table. "My breakfast is getting cold, so if you'll excuse me…"

She waved her hand regally, granting permission. "I ate hours ago. Working women can't lay around like the idle rich."

If her goal was to irritate the hell out of him, she'd succeeded. "Ms. Lassiter," he said coldly, "I was asking you politely to leave."

"Go ahead and ask." She picked up a muffin from the tray and took a bite. "I'm not here to see you." She nodded in the direction of the boy's bedroom. "I came to see him."

"Me?" Thomas's nephew bolted from his room, his hair in spikes and his face glowing. "I'm going with you? Cool."

"Do you know this woman?"

"She's the happy tour lady."

The woman laughed, a throaty, uninhibited laugh. When the women Thomas knew laughed, their high cheekbones didn't press their eyes into thin slits. They avoided wrinkling the skin around their mouths, and they wouldn't be caught dead showing all their teeth. Crunching down on cold, dry toast, he sent his gaze back to the boy and frowned. "Young man, I thought the rule was you are to dress before coming to the breakfast table."

The boy hung his head and drew circles on the carpet with his big toe.

"Maybe his silk robe is in the dirty clothes hamper," the woman said in a cool, disapproving voice.

The early-morning parade of women had thrown Thomas's meticulous habits into total disarray. He'd completely forgotten he still wore his bathrobe. Glaring at her, he curtly ordered the boy to the table. In passing, his nephew shyly smiled up at Cheyenne Lassiter. She tousled his hair.

Thomas shoved one of the straight-backed chairs out from the table. "Sit," he snarled at his uninvited guest.

Her attitude that of one indulging a temperamental child, she complied.

"I want you to tell me—" Thomas slowly hammered out the words "—what the hell is going on."

The swearword won a reproving look from her, then she bounced a glance off the boy. For the first time since he'd opened the door to her, Thomas sensed uncertainty. He opened his mouth to attack.

Cheyenne Lassiter spoke first. "What's your name, kiddo?"

"The boy's name doesn't concern you."

His nephew gave Thomas a wounded glance before staring down at his bowl and muttering, "Davy."

"Nice to meet you, Davy. I'm Cheyenne. As for you, Mr. Steele, you'd be surprised at what concerns me."

He narrowed his eyes at the thinly-veiled animosity in her drawling voice. "Nothing about you would surprise me."

She painstakingly smeared copious amounts of butter on the remains of her muffin. "I'm not sure if that says more about your capacity for surprise or your lack of imagination. Worth claims I give him gray hair." Of course, her brother said that about all three of his sisters.

"Worth? Is he your lov…" Remembering the boy whose head flipped back and forth like a spectator at a tennis match, Thomas smoothly substituted, "Your companion?"

"I wouldn't exactly call Worth companionable."

The crazy notion struck him that Cheyenne Lassiter wanted to goad him into losing his temper. Thomas Steele never lost his temper. The woman took a bite of muffin and chewed deliberately. He ought to kiss that damned smirk right off those damned kissable lips. She was telling the boy she'd read the morning newspaper. As if the boy cared what she read.

"Did you see my ad?"

Belatedly Thomas recalled the newspaper the woman had carried in. "Give me the paper." He assumed she gave dead bugs the same repulsed look. "Please," he ground out.

She handed him the newspaper. Red ink encircled an advertisement.

The boy left his place at the table and edged around to peer over Thomas's arm. "It's in there," he said in an awed voice.

Thomas read the ad. Then read it again. Blood pounded at his temples. "I hope you can explain this, young man."

The boy backed away. "Sandy said."

Thomas recalled the elderly widow who'd seemed so sane and sensible. "Go on," he said grimly. Too grimly. The boy shrugged. Thomas rubbed the back of his neck in frustration. Served him right for impulsively bringing the boy to Aspen. Thomas wasn't in the habit of giving in to impulse.

Cheyenne Lassiter butted in. "What did Sandy say?"

"We was watching this TV program and she said it was too bad I couldn't put a ad in the paper for a mom. I asked her how and she laughed and said Uncle Thomas oughta put one in for a wife and I could live with him. So I asked Tiffany and she said you had to write something and give it to a newspaper. Grandmother gave me money to buy stuff and I asked Paula to take me to the newspaper place."

Thomas couldn't believe the flow of information. He'd

been lucky to pull more than two words at a time from the boy.

"He's not your father?"

"No." The boy looked down at his plate and muttered, "He's Uncle Thomas."

"Why didn't you tell me you weren't his father?"

Trying to recall who, of the horde of females he'd hired to take the boy off his hands, Tiffany was, Thomas merely scowled at her. Paula was the sweet, if not too bright, sister of one of the women at the front desk. Tiffany must be the college student home for the summer.

He eyed his nephew. "I can't believe the newspaper took it without checking with me."

"I said it was a surprise." The boy slid back into his chair. "For your birthday," he added in a barely audible voice.

"My birthday is in April."

The boy dragged his spoon through his oatmeal. "My birthday is in August. Yours coulda been."

Suspicion clawed at Thomas's midsection. "When in August?"

Cheyenne Lassiter glared at him in outrage. "You don't know when your own nephew's birthday is?"

He ignored her, waiting for the boy's answer.

The boy flicked him a look. "August 21. I'm seven."

Three days ago. Thomas clenched his back teeth. Leave it to his mother to neglect to mention the small matter of her only grandson's upcoming birthday. "Finish your breakfast and get dressed."

Thomas stood. "As for you, Ms. Lassiter, despite that ridiculous ad which any halfway intelligent individual would reason was written by a child, I am not seeking a wife." He couldn't throw her bodily out. Not in front of the boy. "I expect you to be gone by the time I finish dressing."

"You didn't eat your breakfast," she pointed out.

"You'll be happy to know you have destroyed my appetite." He stalked across the carpet to his bedroom.

"Then you won't mind if I eat this last muffin. Even Mom's muffins don't compare with St. Chris's. Oh, and Thomas..."

Her low voice invested his name with all kinds of sensual possibilities. He turned. And wished he hadn't.

She studied his legs, then in an exact duplication of his earlier insulting appraisal of her, slowly eyed her way up the length of his body. When at last her gaze reached his face, she gave him a smoldering look from under outrageously long, dark lashes. A muscle in his jaw twitched, and a satisfied smile crawled across her mouth. "I'm not looking for a husband, but if I were, you'd be perfectly safe. Knobby knees really turn me off."

Thomas slammed the bedroom door behind him, catching his bathrobe. A low gurgle of laughter came from the other side of the door. He wanted to rip free the silk garment and shred it into a million pieces. Instead he calmly shrugged out of the robe and let it drop to the floor.

The impassive face on the naked man in the mirror across the room mocked him. His mother had no doubt deliberately neglected to mention the boy's birthday. She'd deny it, of course, turning the blame for not knowing back on him. Damn her.

And damn him for not knowing. Thomas felt like smashing the mirror with his bare fists. Damn. He'd thought he was beyond feeling. Had his family taught him nothing? Damn him for caring. He didn't want to care. Not about the boy. Not about anyone.

A murmur of voices came from the other room. He certainly didn't care that his unwanted visitor despised him. He'd never see her again.

Cheyenne drew open the gold and crimson brocade drapes and brushed aside sheer lace curtains. Through the window's metal mullions, the sight of the gondolas parading up Aspen Mountain reminded her of Thomas Steele. An automated, unfeeling machine.

A machine who'd brought his nephew with him to Aspen.

In her experience, adults who disliked children tried to hide their dislike. Even Harold Karper had publicly pretended a fondness for his stepson.

Thomas Steele demonstrated a total lack of affection for Davy, yet Cheyenne could have sworn he'd been perturbed to learn he'd missed his nephew's birthday. A disconcerting thought crept into her mind, chilling her in spite of the warm, sunny morning. Had Thomas Steele been perturbed, or had she allowed a handsome face to influence her judgment?

Her father had used good looks and a facile charm to sabotage her mother's judgment. Mary Lassiter had paid the price, raising four children by herself while her husband lived a bachelor's life on the rodeo circuit. Calling Beau Lassiter an absentee father overstated his role. Absent, yes. A father, no.

Cheyenne had not been without a loving family. Her mother and grandfather more than made up for Beau's negligence, and Worth and her two sisters would always be there for her.

Davy's parents had died, leaving the poor kid with no one who cared about him. Cheyenne had delicately probed as he ate his breakfast, and the child's artless answers convinced her he wasn't physically battered. The question settled, she should have left when Davy went to his room to dress but the sad lonely picture he painted of an unwanted child, relegated to the periphery of his relatives' lives made her heart ache. She couldn't leave. Not yet.

Cheyenne rubbed the gleaming old oak windowsill. Davy needed a loving family. Someone ought to shake Thomas

Steele until his head snapped. Someone ought to explain to him little boys were more important than hotels and women friends and making money. Her fingernails bit into the sill. She was the only someone around.

"What does a person have to do to get rid of you, Ms. Lassiter? Call security?"

Cheyenne hadn't heard him return. To let him know she considered him quite insignificant, she waited a few seconds before turning to face him. And again felt the impact of his striking dark good looks. If it weren't for the disdain in gray eyes and the cool self-assurance slightly curling the corners of his sensuous mouth, she might have found him attractive. She didn't. Sneering, arrogant males didn't interest her. No matter how tall they were.

She refused to be intimidated by a voice colder than the top of the mountain in February. Even if his beautifully tailored charcoal suit and white-collared dark blue shirt and maroon silk tie made her feel like a slightly grubby adolescent. He looked like a walking advertisement for what the sophisticated businessman should wear if he wanted to radiate power and confidence. And sex appeal.

Thomas Steele straightened a French cuff and lifted an eyebrow, a gesture clearly meant to make her feel like an errant schoolgirl. Cheyenne thrust from her mind any thoughts of his sex appeal. If ever the man existed who needed a few home truths, that man was Thomas Steele.

"I'll leave when I've had my say," she said.

"I'm not interested in anything you have to say."

"Or in Davy or anything he has to say."

"The boy is my business."

"Davy isn't business. He's a little boy. What kind of uncle are you? His parents are dead—yes, he told me. I sat with him while he finished breakfast. You should have. He said he has to stay with you until his grandparents return from a trip. He wanted to go to camp, but you wouldn't let him."

"Six years old is too young for camp."

"He's seven. He had a birthday three days ago, or have you already forgotten again?" If she hadn't been watching closely, she wouldn't have seen the infinitesimal stiffening of his body.

"My family's never put much stock in birthdays."

"Your family doesn't put much stock in family. Davy thinks if he bothers you, you'll lock him in a hotel room by himself."

The barest tightening of his mouth acknowledged her words. "He has too much imagination."

"Does he? I can see he's afraid of you."

"He's afraid of everything. His own shadow, for all I know."

"For all you know. Which isn't very much, is it? He's a little boy, in a strange place, with strange people, and an uncle who does nothing to reassure him. Would it hurt you to sit with him while he eats, talk to him, give him a hug, read him a bedtime story, hear his prayers?"

"It's time he learned there's no such thing as fairy tales, and praying is for those too weak and lazy to stand on their own two feet."

"He's only seven and his parents are dead," Cheyenne said, torn between anger and horror. "He misses them terribly."

"The boy was eight months old when they died. He doesn't remember them."

The quickly vanquished glimmer of pain in his eyes and the tightly controlled voice gave Cheyenne pause. Was Thomas Steele still grieving? Or denying his grief? She chose her words carefully. "Davy said his father was your brother. I'm sorry. It must be awful to lose a brother."

"I don't want your pity."

"Is sympathy for the weak and lazy, too?" The sharp look he gave her should have slashed her to ribbons.

Cheyenne ignored it. "If it doesn't hurt you to talk about your brother, you—"

"It doesn't hurt," he snapped.

"Then why haven't you told Davy about his parents? He knows almost nothing. He said your mother won't talk about them."

Cheyenne wondered what Thomas Steele meant by the harsh laugh he uttered. When he said nothing, she persevered. He doesn't even have a picture of his mother."

"The two of you were certainly chatty."

It would take more than a forbidding, sarcastic voice to chase her away. "He's lonely. The baby-sitters you've hired tell him to go play or sit quietly and watch TV with them. Do you think that's what his parents would have wanted?"

"I have no idea. My brother and I went our separate ways when he married."

"Didn't you like his wife?"

"I never met her. David didn't want me to. He was raised to run Steele hotels, not marry one of the maids. He dropped out of college and out of the family."

"But if he loved her and was happy…"

"Love. Happy." He turned the words into a curse. "Steeles don't marry for love or happiness. They marry for control, power, passion, sex, money and any one of a hundred other reasons, but never for love and happiness." Turning, he walked over to a huge black-lacquered chinoiserie armoire and opened its doors to disclose a fax machine. Ripping off the long ribbon of white hanging from the machine, he began to read.

Actions meant to dismiss her. Cheyenne marched across acres of black floral carpet and sat on the curvaceous purple velvet sofa. "You're a Steele. Is that what you want from marriage?"

"Disappointed?" Looking up from his papers, his grin mocked her. "Did you think I'd take one look at your

frizzy bleached hair and muddy blue eyes and fall hopelessly in love? Forget it. Steeles don't love.''

"Not even little boys?''

"Davy gets fed, clothed and schooled. He'll survive. I
did.''

He'd said the last two words as if they were a badge of
honor instead of extremely sad. If they were true. Studies
proved people needed love to survive. Thomas Steele had
done more than survive. He'd thrived. How convenient to
forget those who had loved him, rather than be inconve-
nienced by his nephew. "Davy needs love and attention,''
she said firmly.

Thomas Steele heaved a long-suffering sigh. "Look, Ms.
Lassiter, lay off the lectures. Bringing the boy was a mistake. Unfortunately I'm stuck with him until his grandparents return.''

Cheyenne traced the patterns in the cut velvet upholstery.
"You cared enough about Davy to worry about him being
too young for camp.''

"Don't read anything into that. You want the brutal
truth, Ms. Lassiter? If my brother hadn't gotten the hots for
a pretty face, we wouldn't have to figure out what the hell
to do with the boy he left behind. Steeles raise hotels, they
don't raise children. Davy would have been better off dying
in the plane crash with his parents.''

The sound of a closing door came on the heels of
Cheyenne's horrified gasp. Thomas Steele instantly spun
around. Jamming his clenched fists into his pockets, he
stared at the closed door to Davy's room. Only the slightest
twitch at the corner of one eye disturbed his stone-carved
countenance. Then he ground out a swearword and turned
away, delivering a swift kick to the nearest chair.

Cheyenne waited until it was apparent Thomas Steele
had no intention of going to his nephew before she went
to Davy's door and knocked. She didn't wait for permission
to enter.

Davy sat on the extreme edge of his bed, his thin shoulders hunched over. Cheyenne sat beside him on the frilly mauve bedspread. Silent tears streamed down his cheeks, answering the question of how much he'd understood of his uncle's words.

When she wrapped an arm around him, Davy tried to pull away, but she held him tighter. With her other hand she reached for a box of tissues and held it out to him. "He didn't mean it." Davy's anguish drew the lie from her. Cheyenne didn't know what Thomas Steele had meant.

"I didn't want to go to camp. There are bears in the woods and I didn't know anybody and I couldn't sleep with my sniffer."

"What's a sniffer?"

Davy hung his head lower. "Grandmother threw Bear away because he had holes and stuff was coming out and she said he smelled bad and I was too old to take him to bed. I saved a little piece that come off. I keep it under my pillow. It's a secret. Pearl knows, but she won't tell."

"Who's Pearl? A friend?"

"She works for Grandmother at the hotel."

"You live in a hotel?"

Davy nodded. Taking a tissue, he noisily blew his nose. "I think Uncle Thomas knows about my sniffer. That's why he don't like me. Pearl said he does, but he don't."

The sad little voice tore at Cheyenne's heart, and she wanted to hit Davy's uncle. Thomas Steele definitely had a problem, and what that problem was, she had no idea, but he had no right to make a little boy so unhappy. Or himself so unhappy. The unbidden thought gave her pause, but Davy came first. Gently squeezing him, she forced lightness into her voice. "Somebody probably took your uncle Thomas's sniffer away from him when he was a little boy and that's why he's so cranky."

Davy gave her a doubtful look. "I don't think he had a sniffer. Grandmother says he's mean and bossy. She told

Grandfather she got the wrong baby when she got Uncle Thomas from the hospital. I asked Pearl what Grandmother meant and she laughed and said Uncle Thomas spits like Grandfather and all the Steeles. I never seen Grandfather spit." He paused. "I thought Uncle Thomas wanted me to come so he could teach me to spit. I'm a Steele, too."

Cheyenne needed a second to interpret Davy's words. "Pearl must have meant your uncle Thomas is the spitting image of your grandfather. That means they look alike. People say my sister Allie and I are the spitting images of each other."

"I wish I had a brother to play with."

Cheyenne saw an opportunity to perhaps repair some damage. "Sisters aren't always so great. Last week Allie let Moonie, one of her dogs, get a hold of my new sweater and Moonie chewed a big hole in it. I told Allie I couldn't decide whether to kill her or Moonie."

Davy gave her a wide-eyed look. "You wanted to kill your sister?"

"Of course not. People say stupid things without meaning what they say. Maybe they are unhappy or in a bad mood. Your uncle's probably in a bad mood because he's hungry." She rubbed Davy's back. "He should have eaten his breakfast."

"Grandmother says I'm a nuisance. When I'm eight she's gonna send me away to school and have a party."

"Your grandmother is teasing you." Inwardly Cheyenne raged. What kind of people were these Steeles?

"He's not," the boy mumbled. "He hates me."

"He doesn't hate you." Cheyenne searched for words to explain Thomas Steele's behavior. How could she explain what she herself didn't understand? Why would a man reject his nephew?

She thought of her own family. Her mother had refused to judge Beau, explaining people had to be taught how to love. Cheyenne had been much older than seven before she understood what Mary Lassiter meant. It wasn't the kind of answer Davy needed now. Feeling her way, Cheyenne said, "You know how it hurts when you fall and cut your knee? Maybe inside, your uncle hurts like that because he misses your father."

"I forgot to feed my goldfish and he died. Grandmother told me I was bad. She flushed Goldie down the toilet." Davy gave Cheyenne a miserable look. "I think I was bad when I was a baby. That's why my mother and father died. That's why Uncle Thomas hates me."

Cheyenne jerked around at a sound behind her. Thomas Steele stood just inside the room.

CHAPTER TWO

"SAY something," Cheyenne said furiously when Thomas Steele did nothing more than imitate a garden statue.

He flicked a stony look at her before saying in a stilted voice, "Your parents died because their plane crashed in bad weather. You had nothing to do with it, and I don't hate you. Don't be dramatic."

So much for sensitivity. Giving Davy another squeeze, she told him to wash his face while she spoke to his uncle. Outside the bedroom, Cheyenne said, "Some reassurance and a hug would have been more appropriate than telling him to quit being dramatic."

A steel beam showed more emotion than Thomas Steele. He stared unblinkingly at her. "I spoke with Frank McCall and he assures me you're legitimate."

"My mother has always said so."

"I'm referring to your business. McCall said you run individual tours for people who don't want to sign up with the usual group tours. He gave you a sterling rating and said he could come up with references if I wanted them."

Cheyenne easily interpreted the begrudging note in Thomas Steele's voice. "Would you have preferred I have a criminal record?"

"You answered the ad for a wife to drum up business."

"I did not."

"Don't waste my time denying it. I admire enterprise. You saw an opportunity and went for it. It worked. You're hired."

"Hired? For what?"

"The women I employed obviously aren't working out. You can take charge of the boy while we're here."

"I run a tour agency, not a day care center."

"McCall said you take kids."

"I take families."

"Drag the boy along."

She'd like to drag someone. Behind a speeding car over a pasture full of cactus. "We run individualized tours for families. Each family pays us to cater to their particular needs and interests. I cannot, as you so crudely suggest, drag a seven-year-old along on a tour personalized for others. It wouldn't be fair to them or to Davy. Aspen has a number of options for day care or activities and tours geared toward children. Frank McCall can steer you to one."

"You came looking for me, Ms. Lassiter, not the other way around. The advertisement brought you, but it was for a wife. Either you came to answer the ad or you came to drum up business. Which?"

The insufferably snapped question enraged her. Cheyenne gave him a cold smile. "I came to see if the child who wrote the ad was being knocked around, battered and physically abused. I came to check for the kind of bruises and broken bones a child receives when someone bigger hits him."

Thomas Steele sucked in air as if she'd kicked him in the solar plexus. "He told you I hit him?" For a second the gray eyes staring at her darkened with baffled hurt. Then he blinked, and his eyes turned cold and empty. "I don't hit people. If he told you I hit him, he lied."

"He didn't tell me. I didn't like the ad."

"I'm not crazy about it myself, but I see it for what it is. A kid with too much imagination and too much time on his hands."

Davy had no bruises, but there were other ways to batter down a child. Believing his family didn't want him ranked right up there. "Is that what you see?" Cheyenne looked directly into the expressionless eyes across from her. "I see a little boy crying out to be wanted and loved."

His mouth tightened and all color left his face, but when he spoke, his voice was coolly impersonal. "I don't have the advantage of your rose-colored glasses."

A person needed years of practice to learn that kind of iron control over his emotions. Cheyenne studied him. "I don't understand how you can be so heartless."

"What's heartless about trying to find a qualified person to take care of the boy?"

"His name is David."

He looked past her. "His father's name was David. The boy's name is Davy."

The way the muscles beneath his jaw tightened made her teeth ache. She'd never seen a man so in denial of his true feelings. Whatever those feelings were. "Then call him Davy," she said, in a gentler tone than she'd intended.

He was quick. One haughty eyebrow identified and mocked her compassion. "You call him Davy. Call him anything you want. All I want is a baby-sitter. Name your price. I'll pay it. I'm not interested in haggling."

Had she been mistaken? You had to be skin and flesh and blood to feel pain. Rawhide and iron and steel formed this man. She questioned the vague plan stirring at the back of her mind. How could words of hers reach him? She should give up now. Walk out of the suite. She couldn't. Davy needed her help. They both needed her help. "I'm not haggling. I'm—"

"Punishing the boy—Davy—because you don't like me."

His accusation angered her. "The world doesn't revolve around you. Your despicable behavior has no bearing on anything."

"I can't imagine you've made much of a success at this little business of yours." Unexpectedly he grinned. "You must find your appalling candor and lack of skill in dealing with people to be terrible handicaps.''

Cheyenne snapped her jaw back into place. It wasn't fair that a man who'd thus far displayed the warmth and compassion of a stone wall could have such an engaging—and sexy—grin. ''You're not a customer,'' she managed.

''I'm trying to be. I want you to take Davy.''

''I get to go with her?'' Davy popped out of his room, his face as hopeful as his voice.

''Ms. Lassiter doesn't want you.''

''Oh.'' Davy disappeared back into the bedroom.

Stunned, Cheyenne stared in disbelief at Thomas Steele. ''Is having your own way so important you'd trample a child's feelings?''

''You're the one who refused to take Davy.'' He jammed his fists in his pockets.

He was going to ruin the line of his expensive suit. He'd said Davy's name. She doubted he'd noticed. If Thomas Steele had any feelings, he'd buried them so deep, he made her think of a tightly-wound spring about to fly out of control. Giving in to impulse, Cheyenne made up her mind. Two lonely people. A little boy who was ready to reach out and a man who apparently could not reach out. All they needed was a little help finding each other. ''There might be a way,'' she said.

Thomas Steele reached for his billfold. ''I knew you'd find one.''

What was she getting herself into? ''How long are you in Aspen?''

''Two more weeks.''

Two weeks. By her estimation, the man had had over thirty years to grow an iron shell, and she expected to pierce it in two weeks? Worth, Allie, Greeley—they'd all shake their heads and accuse Cheyenne of sticking her big nose in other people's business. Again. We all gotta do what we do best, she thought with a grim sense of humor. ''As I said, we run personalized tours. I can't thrust Davy in with strangers doing things which wouldn't interest him. However, Allie's next group canceled because of an illness in the family. I can see if—''

"No," he cut her off. "I don't want Davy shunted off on somebody else. I want you."

He'd said Davy again. The name almost came naturally to him. Maybe there was hope for Thomas Steele. "Most of the families I have booked for the next couple of weeks haven't used us before, and they didn't request me specifically. My sister could take most of them."

"Then it's settled. You'll baby-sit Davy."

"I'm not a baby-sitter, but I'll take Davy. On one condition. You come along."

He slowly returned his billfold to his pocket. "My first guess was correct, wasn't it? It is me you're interested in."

So much for any idealistic plans to turn Thomas Steele into a human being. She gave him a thin-lipped smile. "I can't fool you, can I? All my life I've wanted to be the plaything of a rich, egotistical, sorry excuse for a human being who is absolutely devoid of any kindness, caring, warmth or sensitivity, and I've failed. Let me guess. It's the frizzy bleached hair which turns you off."

Her angry gaze holding his, she called loudly, "Davy, get dressed. You and I are going to go do something fun. Do you like to fish?" She gave Thomas Steele a disgusted look. "I'll need to phone Allie so I can throw her and everyone else's plans into total disarray. Of course, that's nothing to you, as long as you get your way." Without waiting for a response, Cheyenne marched over to the armoire, picked up the phone and dialed for an outside line.

Allie answered on the first ring.

Thomas had had her right where he wanted her—she'd agreed to take the kid out of his hair—and he'd backed down. Thomas Steele, hot-shot businessman with a reputation for driving a hard, fair bargain, who could sit eyeball-to-eyeball for hours over a negotiating table without blinking first, had blinked. The hell of it was, he didn't like any of the possible reasons for why he'd conceded her the victory.

Turning his head, he checked his back cast.

Maybe it was those damned eyes of hers which registered a river of emotions. Anger and contempt. Both better than the disappointment and sadness she'd had the nerve to feel. As if she expected better of him. Not that he cared about hers or anyone else's opinion of him. Even a man scrupulously fair in business dealings stepped on a few toes. A nice fat check took care of hurt feelings or bitterness.

One minute he was patting himself on the back for ridding himself of the kid and the next he was standing thigh-deep in the icy Roaring Fork River wearing hip boots borrowed from Frank McCall. The reason he'd come had nothing to do with Cheyenne Lassiter or the boy. He'd heard her tell Davy they were going fishing and had succumbed to an urge to lay down a line. He'd brought his fly rod with him to Colorado in case an opportunity for fly fishing presented itself. He hadn't actually expected to use the rod. Since he'd bought it five years ago—or was it six, maybe seven?—he'd seldom removed it from its aluminum tube. Running the Steele hotels allowed a man little time for fishing. Or for having a woman in his bed every night. Despite what certain tall blond females thought.

He glanced toward the bank where she sat with the boy. Even from a distance he could tell she still steamed. Ms. Lassiter was easy to annoy. A host of things annoyed her. Not calling the boy by name. Calling her hair bleached. He knew it wasn't, in spite of those dark brows and ridiculously long, black eyelashes. No dark roots.

Bossy blonde. She might have terrific legs, but he detested strong-minded, aggressive women who felt compelled to prove they could be tougher than men. He cast to a likely-looking riffle. It didn't take much imagination to visualize Cheyenne Lassiter in a man's bed. She'd issue such a stream of orders and directives, a man would despair of getting a word in edgewise.

A man could take forever kissing her into silence.

He toyed with the idea of those shapely lips used for something other than lecturing. Those long legs wrapped around him.

He'd always welcomed a challenge.

But he'd never been stupid. It was stupid to seduce a woman merely because she disagreed with you.

The fly floated unchallenged over the riffle. The law prohibited using bait in this section of the Roaring Fork and any fish caught had to be returned immediately to the river. Not that he'd caught any.

Ms. Lassiter hadn't wanted to stop here. She'd argued it wouldn't be fun for Davy. That was her problem. They didn't have to hang around. Thomas had found Davy a playmate. It was up to her to entertain him.

He false cast, drying the artificial fly. Tomorrow he'd tend to business.

And forget self-righteous crusaders who held him in contempt because he didn't behave according to some juvenile, preconceived notions.

Cheyenne Lassiter spent too much time in his head.

A situation he refused to allow. He'd force her out. A woman like her wasn't for a man like him.

Something sharp stung his arm. Rubbing the tender spot, he looked around for biting insects. Another stabbed his back, then a little geyser of water erupted near his legs. A second geyser splashed up. Suspiciously Thomas looked toward the bank, but not in time to evade the sharp object striking his shoulder. He barely avoided the small missile which plopped in the water beside him.

Cheyenne Lassiter dropped her arm when she saw him looking her way. "Hey!" she shouted. "Come over here."

He'd do what he damned well pleased. Thomas carefully waded upstream at an angle to the current, feeling his way around the treacherously smooth rocks. Here, the water ran too fast and deep for Davy's short legs.

A much larger geyser exploded in the water beside him. She'd switched from pea-size gravel to rocks. The woman needed her head examined. A boulder flew through the air, landing harmlessly several feet from him. Effectively scaring off any trout in the vicinity.

Thomas moved a couple of feet closer to the bank so he wouldn't have to holler like someone calling pigs. "I'm trying to fish."

"If you were any kind of fisherman, you'd have caught a fish by now."

He scowled across the water. "No one could catch a fish with you two around. You've done everything but use a bullhorn to frighten the fish away."

"What a self-centered jerk you are."

"When fishing, a man appreciates a little peace and quiet. There's nothing selfish about that."

"You could let Davy try the hip boots."

"I came to fish, Ms. Lassiter, and I intend to fish. Despite your childish behavior." Turning his back, he cast his line upstream.

The rushing river drowned out whatever reply she made. Sunlight sparkled on the water and aspen leaves danced in the breezes, unknotting his muscles. He ought to get away more often. From the office. The hotels. From his family.

Overhead, a commuter jet climbed into the sky from the Aspen airport. Laughter, loud enough to be heard over the river's roar, came from the bank. Thomas looked over his shoulder. Davy, holding the tops of the large rubber boots he wore, splashed in the shallows. The boots must belong to the woman. The boy waded toward the middle of the river. Ms. Lassiter thought she knew everything, but obviously she knew nothing about boys and rocks. Heaving an exasperated sigh, Thomas angled his way downstream toward his nephew.

He'd moved to within several yards of Davy when the inevitable happened. A large, flat rock proving irresistible, the boy scrambled up on it and stepped to the edge furthest from the bank. The fast-moving river had scooped the sand and gravel from beneath the far side of the slick rock, creating a large hole. Davy's weight tipped the rock into the hole and he slid into the river. Thomas dropped his fishing rod and rushed toward his nephew as quickly as he could in the clumsy, borrowed hip boots. Davy was almost in reach when Thomas stepped on a moss-slicked rock and windmilled wildly in the air in a futile attempt to maintain his balance. Falling, he managed to keep his head from slamming onto the river rocks, but icy water cascaded over his shoulders, down his body and poured into the boots. Setting his jaw, Thomas watched Davy splash over.

A big grin covered Davy's face. "I fell in, too, but I didn't get all wet." His grin faded and he took a step back. "Are you mad at me 'cuz you fell in?"

He couldn't look at the boy without scaring him. "I'm not mad at you." It wasn't Davy's fault. Thomas knew who deserved the blame. He sat up, belatedly noting the river was less than six inches deep where Davy had taken his plunge. The only danger Davy had been in, was getting wet. A danger Davy had obviously circumvented much more effectively than Thomas had.

Thomas closed his eyes and slowly counted to ten. He could have counted how many dollars the handcrafted bamboo fly rod speeding downstream to the Colorado River had cost him, but somehow he didn't think that would alleviate his annoyance.

"Are you all right? Did you bump your head?"

He opened his eyes. "No, I did not bump my head," he said coldly to the shapely legs in front of his nose. She'd come in the river wearing her hiking boots. It was her own damned fault if she ruined them.

"Are you hurt? Do you need a hand up?"

"I do not need your help."

"Says you."

"Listen, Ms. Lassiter..." His angry words died away as he looked up. She held his fly rod. Water dripped from the bottom edges of her shorts. "Thank you," he said stiffly.

"Worth would skin me alive if I let an expensive rod like this get away."

Meaning she'd done it for some character named Worth, not for him. Thomas struggled to his feet, taking half the river with him. If she made a single wisecrack, he'd toss her in the middle of the Roaring Fork.

"I have an old pair of Worth's jeans in the car. They're clean and dry. I'll get them." She scrambled up to the parking area, returning seconds later with the jeans.

He grabbed them. "Do you plan to watch me change?" he asked as she stood there.

"Nope. I've seen your knobby knees. C'mon, Davy, let's fix lunch."

Halfway up the bank she slipped and grabbed a clump of weeds at her feet. The sight of her khaki-clad bottom waving in the air momentarily took Thomas's mind off his cold, wet misery.

The jeans were ripped in one knee and threadbare in the other. They were at least a quarter inch too short for Thomas. A fact which, inexplicably, satisfied him immensely.

Cheyenne manfully swallowed her laughter as she poked around in the large basket sitting on the riverside picnic table. Thomas Steele failed to share her amusement at his mishap even after she'd loaned him Worth's dry jeans and given him an old blanket to drape around his shoulders.

Admittedly the river was cold. And wet. She clamped her lips to hold back a giggle.

After he'd changed into Worth's dry jeans, Thomas Steele had marched up the bank on bare feet and ranted and raved, accusing her of all kinds of folly, including recklessly endangering Davy. A person would think Davy had fallen into the middle of the Mississippi River the way his uncle carried on. Cheyenne had kept her mouth shut, not even pointing out that, not only had she never taken her eyes off Davy, she knew to the centimeter the depth of the water where she'd allowed him to play.

Her family would have been astonished at her restraint, Cheyenne had barely listened to Thomas Steele's recriminations. The man could snap and snarl and growl all he wanted, but he'd betrayed himself. Deny his feelings all he wanted, he cared enough about Davy to rush to his rescue. There might be hope for Thomas Steele.

"I'm hungry enough to eat a bear," Davy said.

"A disgusting notion."

Now the man was pouting. "I'm afraid all I have is peanut butter and jelly," Cheyenne said. "No bear."

"Peanut butter and jelly." Thomas Steele grimaced. "I thought you went to the delicatessen."

"Changed my mind. I felt like a peanut butter and jelly sandwich so I went to the grocery store."

"I love peanut butter and jelly sandwiches," Davy said.

"I hate peanut butter and jelly."

"More for us," Davy said with a gap-toothed grin.

"What did you say, young man?"

The snapped question erased the grin on Davy's face. "That's what you said when I told the lady I didn't like fish eggs."

"Those fish eggs were extremely expensive Russian caviar," his uncle said in an overbearing voice. "It would have been more polite to keep your mouth shut. No one forced you to eat caviar."

"What your uncle is saying, Davy, is he holds himself to different standards than he holds you. Children should be seen, not heard."

"I said no such thing, Ms. Lassiter."

"You're absolutely right. All you said was you hated peanut butter and jelly."

"You don't like anyone disagreeing with you, do you?"

"Not when they're wrong, which you are."

He uttered a harsh laugh. "At least you're honest."

"That's me. A frizzy, honest, bleached blonde." More honest than he was. Thomas Steele hid behind so many layers of masks, she questioned if he knew who he was. A cold, selfish uncle or a man hiding from his true feelings? She didn't like the mask he'd shown her. How would she feel about the real Thomas Steele? If one existed.

"If it would make you feel better, I'll admit I rather like your hair, okay?"

As if she cared one tiny bit whether he liked her hair. "It's better than okay. It's better than winning the Colorado lottery. It's better than sunshine and rainbows and chocolate chip cookies." Smearing peanut butter and jelly on two hunks of white bread, she slapped them together and handed him his sandwich.

"I get the picture," he said dryly. "You don't give a damn about my opinion."

Ignoring him, Cheyenne ate her own lunch. A team of wild horses couldn't have dragged from her the admission that peanut butter was not her favorite food, but she'd spent enough time around kids to know what they liked to eat, and she refused to sink to the level of bologna. Chewing resolutely, she used apple juice to wash down the peanut butter gumming up the roof of her mouth. Davy shoved down his lunch and took off to investigate the small gray squirrel scolding them from a large rock beside the river.

Thomas Steele pulled the blanket tighter around his shoulders and turned to lean back against the table's edge.

His eyes closed in the warm sun and his head gradually sank to his chest. Cheyenne sipped juice and studied him. His well-groomed hands were nothing like her brother's. Worth's work-roughened, calloused hands were strong and capable. As was Worth. She wondered about Thomas Steele.

His oblong face softened slightly in repose, although the chin remained as square-cut, the cheekbones as sharp. Not a curl disturbed the blue-black hair laying sleekly over his well-shaped head. A dark, straight brow slashed across his forehead, and a tiny patch of premature gray edged the temple she could see. She approved of the ear lying flatly against his head. His nose fit his face, but his mouth betrayed him with a bottom lip too full for a man. Especially a man who boasted he didn't believe in love.

An urge to touch that lip surprised her. How did he feel about passion?

A hummingbird whistled shrilly past. Thomas Steele stirred, looked up and caught her watching him. His gaze locked on her mouth. Darn him. Was she so transparent?

"Have a boyfriend?" he asked.

"What business is that of yours?"

"You flung around accusations about my social life. Turnabout's fair play. I'll bet you don't. You'd scare off any sane man."

"Do I scare you?"

"Nothing scares me anymore."

"What used to scare you?"

He looked down at the juice bottle in his hands. "Nothing. Where's Davy?"

"Trailing the squirrel. Don't worry. I've been keeping an eye on him while you slept."

"I wasn't sleeping."

"You lie about everything, don't you?"

"Do you have a trust fund or something?"

"What kind of question is that?"

"I'm trying to figure out how you live. No one could support herself with these so-called tours."

"Wait until you get your bill."

"You can't have many repeat customers. People don't care to be lectured to, made fun of, or told they're liars."

"Have I hurt your feelings?" she asked lightly.

"Would you care?"

"No." Maybe poking and prodding him would dislodge his mask. She wanted the real Thomas Steele to stand up.

"Why do I have the distinct impression you want me to lose my temper, Ms. Lassiter?"

"Are you in the habit of losing your temper, Mr. Steele?"

"I don't lose my temper."

"Everyone loses their temper. Do you become violent when you lose yours?"

"Are you deliberately irritating me to see if I'll get mad enough to haul off and slug you?" he asked slowly.

"Will you?"

He gave her a long look. "Don't you think finding out might be a little on the dangerous side?"

"For me? Or for Davy?" After the episode at the river, this man held no terrors for her. He'd fallen, gotten soaked and miserable, and almost lost his fishing rod. He could have blamed Davy for his mishap. Instead he'd lashed out at Cheyenne. That kind of anger grew out of fear. Fear over Davy's safety.

Thomas Steele exhaled impatiently. "I admit the boy and I aren't close. My family isn't exactly your apple pie kind of family, but no one is harming Davy. He's fine."

"He's not fine. He needs parents."

"I can't do anything about that, and I doubt it's true. These days, children are raised by employees and by television. They do fine. Just because your father tucked you in at night doesn't mean every kid needs that."

"I know he's lost his parents, but a child needs someone

who cares about him.'' Cheyenne made a snap decision to tell him a little about herself. ''My father didn't tuck me in. At first he was off rodeoing, then he was just—off. I was ten the last time I saw him.''

''Is that why you hate men? Because you hate your father for abandoning you?''

''I don't hate men and I don't hate my father. He's dead now anyway. Tangled with one bull too many.'' Seeing his blank look, she explained. ''He rode bulls and saddle broncs in rodeos. He was good.'' She flashed a quick smile. ''If he'd been ugly, Mom said even if he could ride anything with four legs, she wouldn't have fallen so hard for him. Or if he was good-looking, but couldn't ride. She claims the combination did her in. Tough, reckless riding and a smile to charm the birds from the trees. When Beau would hobble back with broken bones and his crooked smile, Grandpa would say 'handsome is as handsome does,' and Mom'd laugh and say 'handsome did pretty darned good.' Grandpa always laughed, which made the rest of us laugh. A person couldn't help but like Beau, even if he did shed responsibility the way Shadow sheds water.'' She added, ''Shadow's Allie's black Labrador retriever.''

''You call your father Beau?''

''He didn't like being called Dad.'' Cheyenne made a face. ''Ruined his image.''

''Yet you loved him? How charitable and forgiving of you.''

She heard the sarcasm. ''There was nothing to forgive. Beau never tried to be other than he was. He never promised to come see us or write or phone. He came around when he needed a place for broken bones to heal. He was like an unexpected guest. We'd enjoy him, then he'd leave, and life would return to normal.''

''No resentment at all?'' He clearly doubted her.

''No. We had Grandpa and Mom. And Worth, of course. Beau used to say fate picked Worth's name because Worth was worth ten of Beau." She half smiled. "Beau never lied, not even to himself."

"And you found that admirable, even lovable?" he asked in disgust.

"I'm not stupid, Mr. Steele. I know Beau used his weaknesses to evade responsibility. I liked him. Everyone liked Beau. But love?" She shook her head. "Love is for men like Grandpa and Worth. Men you can depend on. None of us kids loved Beau. We accepted him." She drew in the dirt with a stick. "That's sad, don't you think? Beau had excitement and glamour and women and a certain amount of fame. He never had kids who loved him."

"Sounds as if he had what he wanted."

"Beau didn't know what he wanted. He grew up in a series of foster homes. Beau never saw his mom, but for some reason, she never signed the papers which would allow him to be adopted. As a result, he never connected with anyone. He didn't know how to love." Cheyenne watched Davy standing beside the river looking up into the branches of a small aspen. "A child has to be loved to learn how to love."

"I had a feeling your true confession was leading somewhere. Forget it. I'm no more interested in your opinions on child-rearing than I am in hearing your family's history."

"Why do you deny Davy what you had? Parents and family who loved you?" Cheyenne asked in a quiet, intense voice.

"Don't forget the hundreds of gorgeous women who are madly in love with me and nightly grace my bed." He paused. "Considering your appalling naïveté, I ought to assure you they grace it one at a time."

His patronizing smile went no further than his lips. His eyes told her nothing. He hid his secrets well. He hadn't answered her question. His jaw tightened. Her scrutiny bothered him. She wondered what kind of parents he'd had, but knew better than to ask.

Thomas gave a low laugh. "The next time you start on one of your dreary little sermons, I'll remember that mentioning my sex life shuts you up."

The triumph in his voice saddened her. Life was about winning and losing to him, and he thought he'd won. Perhaps he had. Only an idiot would believe she could turn this man and Davy into a family. Allie was right. Cheyenne couldn't save the world.

She could give Davy a friend for two weeks. After that... Cheyenne wrapped her arms around herself and watched Davy stalk a butterfly through a small patch of fuchsia-blooming thistles. "I'll pick Davy up at eight-thirty tomorrow morning."

Thomas Steele said nothing. The silence grew. She wanted t~ cry and scream and throw things and kick her feet in frustration. Why couldn't he understand? Tiny prickles crawled down her spine. Raising her chin, she turned her head.

He was studying her, an enigmatic look on his face. "He'll be ready."

She'd missed something. He seemed almost disappointed. As if he'd expected something else from her. Something more. Surely not jealousy at the thought of other women in his bed. So what her knees went a little weak at the sight of the chest he'd exposed to the sun's rays? It took more than blatant masculinity to offset bony knees.

He closed his eyes, shutting her out. Silly thought. When had he let her in? The feeling he'd wanted something from her and she'd failed to deliver wouldn't go away. Maybe she hadn't been clear enough. Surely he understood she'd agreed to take Davy for the next two weeks. Didn't Thomas Steele realize she was letting him off the hook?

An incredible thought almost knocked her off the picnic table bench. Perhaps Thomas Steele didn't want off the hook. The outline of a brilliant plan sprang into being. What if she refused to let him off the hook?

Deciding to put her theory to the test, Cheyenne spoke before sanity prevailed. "I'll take Davy to the Aspen Center for Environmental Studies in the morning. We can kill a couple of hours at the nature preserve watching the hawks and ducks, look for a muskrat or beaver. Will that be enough time for you to get things ready for the party?"

Thomas Steele's eyelids snapped up. "What party?"

"Davy's birthday party. I'll order the cake tonight and you can go shopping for presents and decorations in the morning."

"His birthday has passed."

"A late party is better than no party."

"Fine. Give him a birthday party and send me the bill. I don't care how you entertain him."

Cheyenne chose to misinterpret his words. "If you don't care what kind of party, I have a better idea. Mom and Worth would think it great fun to throw a birthday party at Hope Valley. I'd planned to go out to the ranch tomorrow afternoon, but we can go earlier. Mom loves to bake birthday cakes. I'll take Davy with me to buy the ice cream and decorations and tell him they're for Worth. You'll be in charge of the presents."

Thomas Steele looked at her as if she'd grown several extra heads. He opened his mouth, but Cheyenne had no intention of giving him an opportunity to refuse. "A couple of hours should give you enough time. We'll come back to the hotel for you and Olivia. She's booked with Allie for tomorrow, and she'll love a party."

"Ms. Lassiter." He stood. The blanket fell to the picnic bench. "I'm not—"

"You'll like Olivia," Cheyenne said quickly, trying not to stare at the sculpted male torso shining in the sunlight. "She's filthy rich, and she always stays in Steele hotels."

He moved to stand in front of her. "I'm not interested

in meeting this woman no matter where she stays or how much money she has. Or how beautiful she is.''

"I'm not fixing you up." If he moved much closer, her nose would bump the bare skin above Worth's old jeans. He wanted to make her nervous. He couldn't. "Olivia's eighty-three." The day had grown warmer. Cheyenne resisted an urge to fan her face with her hat. The sun was going to burn his broad shoulders and blister the wide expanse of skin. Not that she cared. He could strip stark naked and it wouldn't bother her.

"Definitely not my type."

Of course she wasn't his type. "What is your type?"

"A woman younger than eighty-three."

He was talking about Olivia. She knew that. "You're Olivia's type." He was leaner than Worth. The jeans hung low on his hips. She tried not to stare at his flat stomach. "She's crazy about men who are tall, dark, handsome and devastatingly sexy."

Hands came to rest on her shoulders. "How about you, Ms. Lassiter? What kind of men are you crazy about?" He laughed, low in his throat, and pulled Cheyenne to her feet. "I'm flattered you think I'm devastatingly sexy."

CHAPTER THREE

CHEYENNE could not believe the incriminating words had come from her mouth. She put up her hands to ward him off, then snatched them away, conscious of the warmth of his chest. Curling her fingers at her sides, she looked in the direction of the shirt and fishing vest spread over a nearby wild rose bush. "I think your shirt is dry."

"I like a woman who thinks I'm devastatingly sexy." His mouth hovered inches above hers.

She took a deep breath and forced herself to meet his eyes. "I meant Olivia will think you are, and that's what counts. I like to keep my clients happy."

"I'm your client."

"Davy's my client."

"I'm paying the bill. A bill you've assured me will be quite high." He slid one hand across her shoulder. "Maybe you ought to think about keeping me happy."

Cheyenne didn't make the mistake of thinking Thomas Steele was interested in her. Seduction was merely another mask he hid behind. Not about to swoon at his feet, she slipped beneath his arm. "All I have to do to keep you happy is keep Davy out of your hair. Don't read anything in my comment about your personal appearance. Good looks are nothing more than the luck of the draw from the gene pool."

"And that means good looks aren't sexy?"

She elected to answer him honestly. "You want to know what's sexy in a man? Goodness, caring, gentleness. Kindness."

"I suppose this Worth you talk about is sexy."

43

"Worth? Sexy?" Cheyenne burst out laughing. "He'd throw a fit if I even suggested it."

"He's not good and kind and gentle?"

Cheyenne cleared up the remains of the lunch. "Of course he is." She'd contradicted her own words. "But Worth is just Worth." She closed the lid to the picnic basket, puzzling over Thomas Steele's tone. For whatever reason, he'd sounded almost petulant when he'd said Worth's name. Which made no sense.

Unless men were like bull elk in the fall. Macho, competitive, and determined to be the number one bull. Maybe she could use male testosterone to Davy's advantage. "Of course," she said casually, "Worth is good-looking, and I have to admit his blue eyes are gorgeous. Half the women in the valley are in love with him. You wouldn't believe the stupid reasons they give for showing up at our ranch so they can see him. My sister claims his muscles turn the average woman's brain to mush."

Thomas Steele grabbed the picnic basket. "I'll carry it. Open the back end of your car." He slid the basket inside and slammed the back of her vehicle. "It sounds to me as if there are too many distractions for you on your ranch. I don't think Davy should go with you tomorrow. You almost lost him today in the river. He could get into all kinds of trouble on a ranch while you're otherwise occupied."

"I did not almost lose him in the river. He was in no danger whatsoever. And you don't have to worry about him on the ranch. Worth will take care of Davy."

Thomas Steele carefully gathered up the gear air-drying on a rock in the shade. "I'll decide who takes care of him."

"Naturally." Cheyenne signaled Davy to head for the car. "He is your nephew."

Thomas Steele gave her a measured look. "I am not going to help you with your so-called birthday party. I have no idea what a seven-year-old boy would like."

"It doesn't take a brain surgeon to figure out. What did

you do at your birthday parties when you were Davy's age?''

After a moment he said, ''I never had a birthday party.''

The bald statement gave Cheyenne pause. She couldn't help picturing Thomas Steele as a child, pretending year after year that birthday parties didn't matter. Her heart twisted, and she wanted to hold him in her arms and console the child he'd been. Before she made a fool of herself, Davy ran up, flying his uncle's shirt behind him like a flag.

''Are we gonna fish now?'' Davy asked.

Thomas Steele took his shirt. ''I'm going back to the hotel. I have work to do.''

''Oh.'' Davy scuffed his toe in the dirt. ''I thought you was gonna fish with me. I guess you don't want to.''

Thomas Steele gripped his shirt so tightly, his knuckles turned white. ''It has nothing to do with you. There are things which need to be done.''

''Let someone else do them,'' Cheyenne said. If Thomas Steele wanted to return to St. Chris's, he'd have to get there on his own. ''I booked you for the whole day. We're going to Ruedi Reservoir so you can teach Davy how to fish.''

Disappointment switched to hopefulness on Davy's face. ''We are? Cool.'' He gave his uncle a sideways glance. ''I'll prolly catch a fish.''

Thomas Steele raised an eyebrow at his nephew. ''Are you casting aspersions on my fishing ability, young man?''

Davy stood his ground. ''I don't know,'' he said cautiously. ''What does that mean?''

''You think I'm not a very good fisherman.''

''You didn't catch any fish.''

Cheyenne laughed.

Thomas Steele swung his gaze toward her. ''I see there are two of you who think I don't know anything about fishing. All right, we'll have a little contest. Biggest fish wins.''

''What will I win?'' Davy asked excitedly.

"You're awfully confident, young man."

"Pearl told me Steeles always think big," he said seriously. "I'm a Steele."

His uncle's face stilled. "More's the pity," he said tonelessly.

Cheyenne jumped in before Davy worked out the meaning of his uncle's cryptic words. "I'm not a Steele, and I intend to win this contest." She eyed Thomas Steele thoughtfully. "I think the winner should select her prize."

"If I win," Davy asked, "can I wear the wading boots?"

"If you win." Thomas Steele's gaze went to Cheyenne's lips. "I plan to win and I have something else entirely in mind. Something I intend to enjoy to the fullest."

Cheyenne forgot to breathe. There was no misinterpreting his words and look. He planned to kiss her. If he won. She inhaled deeply. "Don't count your chickens before they're hatched."

He gave her a lazy smile. "I love barnyard clichés. There's something so—" he lifted his brow in an exaggerated leer "—earthy about them."

Cheyenne would have laughed. If she could have. If he hadn't reached back at that exact second to slide an arm into the sleeve of his shirt. If his bare chest hadn't stretched and flexed. If his words hadn't conjured up a sudden vision of the two of them on the ground wrapped in an embrace. Not a single thought or word came to her rescue. Turning on her heel, she went around her car and jumped in the driver's seat. Her breathing had almost returned to normal by the time everyone had strapped in.

Thomas Steele had provided her with a double incentive to win. If she won, she intended to make him participate in Davy's birthday party. Even more important, if she won, she wouldn't have to kiss Thomas Steele. She didn't have the least bit of curiosity about his kisses.

Cheyenne knew exactly what Thomas Steele was doing. Punishing her for forcing him to spend the day with his nephew. Punishing her for daring to condemn his care of his nephew. Punishing her for not accepting his own highly-elevated opinion of himself. For all she knew he was even punishing her for the pizza he'd eaten. Not that his supper was any more her fault than him spending the day with his nephew. He was the one who decided to go fishing with them. She'd told him he didn't have to eat with them. That she'd deliver Davy back to the hotel after supper. But no, he couldn't do that. Not when he knew darned good and well every second in his company further irritated the heck out of her.

He'd been lucky.

That big, stupid trout had by-passed her salmon egg and Davy's marshmallow and gone for Thomas Steele's artificial fly. The dumb fish was all brawn and no brain. No wonder Thomas Steele had tossed it back in the water. She wished she could toss Thomas Steele back.

She knew he planned to kiss her. He knew she knew. He could have kissed her as soon as he'd caught the monster fish. They'd all known the trout was a winner.

He could have kissed her before they'd started back to Aspen. He could have kissed her when they'd pulled up to St. Chris's or before they'd gone into the hotel.

Thomas Steele preferred to torment her. To prolong her dread. To keep her dangling, wondering when he'd kiss her.

If he'd kiss her.

Cheyenne screeched to a halt in the middle of St. Chris's lobby. He didn't want to kiss her. She had peanut butter breath. He'd never intended to kiss her. A man like Thomas Steele didn't kiss an insignificant nobody like Cheyenne Lassiter.

Wait a minute. She was too good for an insufferable egotist like Thomas Steele, even if he was one of the hotel Steeles. She was one of the ranching Lassiters, wasn't she?

"So you told me," Thomas Steele said dryly. "What about it?"

Heat stained her cheeks. She hadn't intended to say the words out loud. "Nothing about it." She looked around the three-story atrium lobby. Davy was regaling two of the bellmen with the story of his day's adventures. From the way he held his hands, she guessed he was telling them about his uncle's fish. "It wasn't that big," she muttered.

"Bigger." Thomas Steele had followed her gaze.

"You were in such a hurry to throw it back, I didn't get a good look at how big it was." She knew the sooner a fish was released back into water, the better its chance of survival. "My fish might have been bigger."

He grinned. "Your fish wasn't half the size of mine. Even Davy's fish dwarfed yours."

She hated it when he grinned. Standing there in Worth's ragged jeans, bare feet shoved in athletic shoes, he ought to look ridiculous. The hotel staff was too well-trained to laugh out loud, but they must be snickering behind their hands. She wanted to laugh at him, mock him. He played so unfair. Catching the biggest fish. Grinning at her. Messing with her insides. "I'm not going to kiss you."

His grin widened. "Who asked you to?"

She didn't care how sexy-looking he was, he was a conceited pain in the neck. "If you won, you expected me to kiss you."

"I said that?"

"Maybe you didn't say it." She felt like twisting off his ears. "You know very well you implied it."

Stepping closer, he captured the ringlets pulled through the back of her baseball cap. "How did I imply it?"

She didn't like the way his eyes laughed at her. Or the way he brushed her neck with the ends of her hair. "You looked at me." Even to her, the words sounded stupid.

Thomas Steele laughed out loud.

Every head in the hotel turned in their direction.

Cheyenne's face flamed. "Let go of my hair. I have to go talk to Olivia about tomorrow."

"I thought you wanted to kiss me."

"I do not want to kiss you." She pulled at his hand. He hung on to her hair. "Everyone's staring at us. Let go. I live in Aspen. People know me."

"Do they know you welsh on a bet?" He shook his head in mock reproach. "And you a Lassiter of the ranching Lassiters."

"I'm not welshing, but I'm not going to kiss you in the lobby of St. Chris's."

"You're right. If you want to kiss me, there are better places than a hotel lobby."

"I don't want to kiss you." Cheyenne took a deep, exasperated breath. "All right, what did you want for a prize if you caught the biggest fish?"

His hand tightened on her hair. "My mother brought me up to be a gentleman. Forget what I wanted. A lady's wish is my command. Since you want me to kiss you..."

He'd quit smiling. The voices around them faded away. His eyes held hers in a manner which was less seductive than challenging. As if daring her to kiss him in the middle of the lobby. Her breathing grew shallow and tension prickled in her breasts. She wasn't going to kiss him. Not here. Maybe upstairs. In his suite. After Davy went to bed.

Bed. The word acted as a brake, and Cheyenne drew back her head. Thomas Steele smiled. Whatever kind of contest they'd been engaged in, he knew he'd won. She wanted to kick him right in the middle of his bony knees. He may have caught the biggest fish, but he darned well wasn't going to win this battle, whatever it was about. "I won't force a kiss on you," she said. "Tell me what you planned to ask for if you won."

"I forget. Give me a kiss, and we'll call ourselves even."

She'd never be even with this man. He was too accustomed to having the upper hand. As he thought he did now.

She had to beat him at his own game. "All right. One kiss. And no more talk of welshing. Agreed?"

"Agreed." He slid the bill of her cap sideways and lowered his head.

Cheyenne rose to her tiptoes and brushed a quick kiss against his cheek. The feel of his warm skin, rough with stubble, shook her to the soles of her walking shoes. "There," she managed to say.

He rubbed his cheek. "That wasn't in the spirit of the bet."

She forced herself to meet his gaze. "You insisted on a kiss. You got a kiss. If you had a particular type of kiss in mind, you should have specified."

"Next time I won't leave you any loopholes."

"There won't be a next time. It's going to be just Davy and me." A circumstance she regretted. Not for her. She certainly didn't want to kiss him again. She didn't care two beans if she ever saw Thomas Steele again.

She regretted for Davy's sake. Davy desperately needed someone to love him, to parent him. From what he'd told her about his grandparents, they weren't giving him what he needed.

Cheyenne had hoped if Thomas Steele spent a day with Davy away from the hotel, he'd see how much his nephew needed him. And realize how much he needed Davy. Neither had happened.

"Goodbye, Mr. Steele." Cheyenne extended her hand. "If you need to contact me, or have any questions or instructions about Davy, call my answering machine or leave a message here with the front desk. Don't worry about Davy. He'll have a great time, and I'll take good care of him."

He held her hand instead of shaking it. "It's better this way, Ms. Lassiter. You'd want more than I'm capable of giving."

Cheyenne looked down at her hand enclosed in his. "Davy doesn't want so much. He'd be easy to love."

"The only way Davy enters in to what I'm talking about is if he weren't here, things would be different with you and me."

"You wouldn't be hiring me to entertain him."

"No, I'd be seriously considering whether I wanted you to entertain me while I'm here."

There was no misinterpreting his words. She yanked her hand free. "I'm sure you can find plenty of women interested in entertaining you, Mr. Steele. You're not my type."

"Precisely my point. You're the wholesome, down home, small town type of woman who believes in love and commitment. I prefer women from the fast lane."

"I'm not the least bit interested in your likes and dislikes. Or in you."

He half smiled. "You're as curious as I am about what would happen if we really kissed."

She wasn't curious. She knew. His kiss would be cataclysmic. Obviously Thomas Steele had not received the same jolt of electricity. Not that it mattered.

"No point in speculating about something that's never going to happen, Mr. Steele." Assuming her business face, she said briskly, "I'll shop for tomorrow. I think the best way to handle the bills is for me to pay for everything and at the end of Davy's stay, I'll present the receipts along with my bill."

"Handle it however you wish," he said in a bored voice.

Disappointment flooded Cheyenne. He'd switched back to the unreachable Thomas Steele he'd been this morning. There ought to be something she could say. Something to magically turn Thomas Steele into a human being. To make him understand how much Davy needed him. How much he needed Davy. To make him see how rich his life could be. He didn't want to see. A sensible woman would forget about turning Thomas Steele and his nephew into a real family.

"Tommy."

The elegantly-modulated voice pulled Cheyenne from her frustrated thoughts, and she turned to see a tall, thin woman with sleek, dark auburn hair glide across the lobby's marble parquet floor. Enough gold jewelry to pay off the national debt hung around the woman's swanlike neck. She had perfectly arched eyebrows, perfect skin, and perfect makeup. The latest perfect shade of lipstick had been perfectly applied to perfect lips. Only a shallow man would find such artificial perfection appealing. Cheyenne started to walk away.

"Wait." Thomas Steele wrapped his long, elegant fingers around her wrist. "A change of plans may be called for."

If Thomas Steel thought he would be doing her a favor by throwing this woman's business her way, he could think again. Cheyenne had been in the tour industry long enough to know she wanted nothing to do with Ms. Perpetually on a Diet. Nobody could satisfy this type, and Cheyenne had no intention of trying.

The woman's numerous rings included no wedding ring. Divorced. Which explained the look, half sultry and half predatory, on her face. The woman was on the hunt, and Thomas Steele, Tommy, was her target.

Tommy. He looked as much like a Tommy as Cheyenne looked like a wealthy socialite. No wonder his acknowledging smile failed to get as far as his eyes.

The woman took her time reaching them. One couldn't rush and glide at the same time. She halted in front of Thomas Steele. Cheyenne had never seen a woman smile without creasing any part of her face.

"Surprise, Tommy."

"Stephanie."

"I was bored to tears with you out of town." The woman

pushed out a reddish-brown bottom lip. ''When Bobby and Cynthia Jones told me they were flying to Aspen... You remember Robert Pennelton Jones, don't you, Tommy? Of the Manhattan Penneltons. He does something with money on Wall Street.''

''Makes it, no doubt,'' Cheyenne couldn't resist saying.

One thin arched eyebrow arched higher. ''You know the Joneses?'' Her voice expressed doubt as she took in Cheyenne's clothes, but left room for the possibility Cheyenne might be someone worth knowing.

''I never bother to keep up with the Joneses.'' Her wrist burned where Thomas Steele held it. Cheyenne had the crazy impression he held on to her the way a drowning man clings to a life preserver.

''How amusing your little friend is.'' The temperature in the lobby dropped ten degrees as the skinny redhead dismissed Cheyenne. Focusing on Thomas Steele, she re-upped the voltage. ''What fun to run into you, Tommy. Of course, you'll join us for dinner and night-clubbing tonight, and then—'' she lowered her voice seductively ''—who knows?''

''Thank you, Stephanie, but I've dined.''

''You can't possibly have. It's only seven.''

''As I told you in New York, my nephew is with me. Cheyenne insists we let Davy set our schedule. Cheyenne, this is Stephanie Winston. Stephanie, Cheyenne Lassiter.'' His mouth barely twitched. ''One of the ranching Lassiters.''

The woman acknowledged the introduction in a voice as insincere as Cheyenne's. A quick sweeping look took in Thomas Steele's hand wrapped around Cheyenne's wrist before she said in a flirtatious manner, ''Tommy, you're too good to the child. He can spare you while he sleeps. It would be too bad if you missed Bobby and Cynthia and missed hearing all the latest news from our crowd.'' Stephanie Winston turned a saccharine smile Cheyenne's way. "You'll be a darling and stay with the child while Tommy joins us for a few drinks, won't you?"

"She can't," Thomas Steele spoke first. "Cheyenne and Davy and I have big plans for tomorrow, so we need to call it an early night." He dropped Cheyenne's wrist to slide his arm around her waist. "Isn't that right, Cheyenne?"

"Isn't Cheyenne a cowboy town in Wyoming?"

Cheyenne disliked the disdainful tone of Ms. Winston's voice almost as much as she disliked Thomas Steele's arm around her waist. "Yup," she drawled, "my daddy named all us buckaroos after rodeos. I'm named after Cheyenne Frontier Days."

"How quaint."

"More like convenient, what with Daddy not around much, except when he got stove-up by some no-account, notional bull. Then he'd come sniffing around Ma's skirts, and bingo, there'd be one more of us. Daddy was better at remembering winning than kids' names, so Ma thought us kids should be like silver belt buckles. We all stand for Daddy's best rides. Daddy thought she ought to name us for the bulls, but Ma put her foot down. Good thing, or I'd be Blizzard Babe."

Thomas Steele lightly slapped her bottom. "Behave yourself." His hand stayed on her hip. "Cheyenne takes a perverse sort of pride in keeping secret the fact that she graduated from Princeton."

Cheyenne managed to conceal her surprise. Frank McCall, St. Chris's manager, must have detailed her entire life history. He should have added that being used to deflect predatory women didn't come under a tour agent's job description. Thomas Steele would pay for using her.

Leaning her hip against his, Cheyenne smiled at the woman glaring at her. "Thomas is so much fun to tease. I'm sure I don't have to tell you that." She transferred her smile to Thomas. "I think tomorrow our bet ought to be double or nothing." Her gaze returned to Stephanie

Winston. "Don't you hate it when Thomas wins? He gloats. Would you believe he made me kiss him right here in the middle of St. Chris's lobby?"

Ms. Winston lifted her eyebrows. "The way you're dressed, Tommy, I'd have guessed you lost a bet."

Cheyenne giggled. She hadn't giggled since junior high school. "We were messing around by the river and he fell in. He had to remove every single stitch of clothing."

"How unfortunate."

"Thomas is tough. The only thing he complained about is eating peanut butter and jelly sandwiches. Which Davy and I agree is better than eating fish eggs...oh...I hope you're not the woman who likes caviar."

"Cheyenne, we'd better collect Davy and go up to our suite. Enjoy your stay, Stephanie. Since I won't be able to join you and your friends this evening, I hope you'll accept a bottle of champagne, courtesy of the hotel. Nice to see you. Davy!" He swept Cheyenne around an ornate metal column and across the lobby.

She went along. Doing so fit nicely with her plans. In a voice meant to reach Ms. Winston, Cheyenne said, "That wasn't the woman Davy told me about, was it? Why didn't you stop me? Thank goodness I didn't repeat what you said." Conscious of the woman watching them as they reached the elevators, Cheyenne angled around and wrapped her arms around his neck. Plastering an intimate smile on her face, she said softly, "If you don't come with us tomorrow, I'll toss you to her. Hog-tied and ready for branding."

In spite of his hands resting on her hips, Thomas's smile lacked warmth. "Threatening me, Ms. Lassiter?"

"Is it a threat?" She couldn't resist. "Tommy."

"Were you really named for a rodeo?"

Her breathing quickened as his thumbs drew slow circles over her shorts. "I thought Frank McCall gave you my life history."

"He would have."

"If you'd been interested."

His thumbs stopped. "If I'd been interested."

"Do you know Ms. Winston's life history?"

"Jealous?"

"Only of her plastic surgeon."

"You are jealous." Speculation filled his eyes. "Interesting."

"We won, didn't we, Uncle Thomas?" Running up, Davy gave his uncle a comradely grin. "Us guys beat Cheyenne."

Thomas Steele went very still, his gaze locked on his nephew's beaming countenance. "Yes, we won," he said in a distracted voice.

"How cum Cheyenne kissed you?"

"Because she lost." Thomas Steele reached down as if to touch Davy's shoulder, then yanked back his hand and shoved it in his pocket.

His refusal to admit he cared for Davy made her want to cry. Clearing her throat, Cheyenne said the first thing she could think of. "I hate losing and I hate kissing. It makes me sick."

Thomas Steele gave her a mocking smile. "Anyone who likes peanut butter sandwiches has a cast-iron stomach."

His armor was securely back in place. Sighing inwardly, Cheyenne said, "For peanut butter and jelly. Not for kissing."

The elevator arrived and Thomas Steele pressed her into the wood-paneled compartment, his hand warm against her back. Cheyenne stared at the flowery metal fittings near the ceiling and wished St. Chris's had larger elevators.

Davy followed them in and the door slid shut. "Uncle Thomas, don't kissing girls make you sick?"

"No. It's like peanut butter and caviar. When you're

young you like peanut butter. When you're older, you like caviar.''

"Cheyenne is old and she likes peanut butter.''

Cheyenne playfully socked Davy's shoulder. "Thanks, kiddo.''

"Let me tell you about women, Davy,'' his uncle said. "They don't like it when you call them old.''

Davy turned to Cheyenne. "Why don't you want to be old? I wish I was old like Uncle Thomas.''

"Why?'' Cheyenne asked.

"'Cuz he's tall and gets to do what he wants and he knows everything and nothing scares him.''

Cheyenne knew budding hero worship when she heard it. The uncomfortable look on Thomas Steele's face told her he'd reached the same conclusion.

The elevator stopped, and the door opened. Cheyenne pushed the button to hold the door open. "Since you beat me, too, I guess I'll have to kiss you,'' she teased Davy.

"No!'' Davy dashed from the elevator and tore down the hall.

"Aren't you coming?'' Thomas Steele asked.

She shook her head. "I'm going to Olivia's room. She'll want to hear what the four—'' she accentuated the number "—of us are doing tomorrow. Tommy.''

"Blackmail, Ms. Lassiter?''

"Absolutely.'' Cheyenne fluttered her eyelashes in a parody of flirtatiousness. "Tommy.'' She pressed the button for Olivia's floor. "See you tomorrow. I'll fax you your shopping list, Mr. Steele.''

He stopped the door from closing. "If you're going to blackmail me, Cheyenne, you ought to call me Thomas.''

"All right. Thomas.''

"And you might want to cool it with the flirting. I wouldn't object to you in my bed. Be careful what you start. I won't be adverse to finishing it.'' He stepped back.

"If you're trying to scare me so you can get out of going

with us tomorrow, forget it.'' The doors shut and the elevator started down. "You can't scare me."

He couldn't.

What she wanted from him had nothing to do with kisses. She wanted him to take Davy into his heart. Not her into his bed.

Thomas knew that.

He was no more interested in her than she was in him, but he didn't like her criticizing his treatment of Davy. She knew what he was doing. He considered her a pest, and the best way to get rid of pests was to chase them off.

He couldn't chase her off with vague warnings of being physically attracted to her. Cheyenne stepped from the elevator on Olivia's floor. Men like Thomas didn't make her nervous. The unsettled sensations in her stomach came from the excessive amounts of cheese on the pizza. She'd weathered queasy stomachs before. Her stomach felt better already, and her recovery had nothing to do with leaving Thomas Steele one floor above.

She knocked on Olivia's door. "It's me, Cheyenne."

After a few minutes the door opened. Bent over her walker, Olivia gave Cheyenne a broad smile. "I saw you in the lobby. Get right in here and tell me all about that handsome man you kissed." She clutched her chest dramatically. "My heart is still palpitating just from looking at him. My granddaughter would call him a real sexy hunk. I'd swoon if he smiled at me like he smiled at you." Her smile switched to a frown. "What's the matter? All of a sudden you look a little funny."

"The peanut butter I had for lunch is warring with the pizza I had for supper. That's all it is." Talking about Thomas Steele and his stupid hunkiness didn't affect her at all.

Thomas strolled down the hall toward his suite. Remembering the panic in Cheyenne's eyes made him want to laugh. She could deny it all she wanted, but she was definitely interested.

"I gotta go." Davy hopped up and down in front of the door.

Thomas quickened his pace.

Once in the suite, he crossed to the armoire, checked his messages and looked over the stream of paper hanging from the fax machine. Nothing urgently required his attention. He poured himself a glass of wine and stretched out on the purple velvet sofa. Setting the stemmed glass on his chest, he closed his eyes, shutting out his surroundings.

He preferred checking into a different room each time he stayed at a Steele hotel. His grandmother claimed the only way to discover a hotel's shortcomings was to stay in a room not preselected by the hotel staff.

Unfortunately, his mother didn't share that wisdom, and since his grandmother's death all Steele hotels had a suite set aside for family use. Each "done" by whatever New York decorator happened to be in vogue at the time. The St. Christopher Hotel's other hotel rooms reflected the original owner's choice of Art Nouveau architecture. Thomas couldn't settle on the style of this suite. Maybe eclectic. Or decorator on drugs.

He took a sip of wine. It tasted surprisingly good. The wine had come from northwestern Colorado. A wine didn't have to be European to be drinkable, but he'd questioned McCall's judgment in stocking Colorado wines when they had so little history. This wine was eminently drinkable. He'd have to congratulate McCall. Tourists liked the idea of eating and drinking local products.

Thomas took another sip. Spicy. Slightly tart. Piquant. Unassuming, yet challenging. No pretensions to being other than what it was.

Like Cheyenne Lassiter.

Thomas prided himself on never lying to himself and he didn't lie now. He wanted her.

Any number of women would happily jump into his bed. He toasted himself. "To the CEO of the Steele Hotels." He owned a mirror. He knew what women saw when they looked at him. He also knew his appearance wouldn't mean a thing if the women didn't sense an aura of power and money clinging to him.

Cheyenne Lassiter couldn't care less about his aura. He didn't come up to her standards. Not like this Worth character she set up among the gods. Thomas took a swallow of wine and considered whether she slept with this Worth. He didn't think so. Something about her eyes. Her awareness of himself. Her shallow, quickened breathing when they stood close. He smiled. She wanted him.

Draining his glass, Thomas analyzed why he wanted her. He'd seen more beautiful women. Met more intellectual women, richer women, more powerful women. Known nicer, sweeter women. She didn't even like him.

Sitting up, he reached for the wine bottle and refilled his glass. Sexual awareness wasn't the only thing he read in her eyes. She wanted him to love Davy, and he couldn't. Her condemnation of that failure spilled from her eyes.

Who was she to judge him? Even worse was the pity. Damn her for daring to pity him.

He poured another glass of wine. If he had her beneath him, nothing between them but skin, her bare, long legs wrapped around him, he'd soon make sure her eyes reflected nothing but the pleasure he gave to her.

Thomas discarded the fantasy. He had no intention of falling into bed with Cheyenne Lassiter. The hell with her. He wouldn't go tomorrow. She and Davy could celebrate without him.

He didn't want Davy depending on him. Growing close to him. He'd let him down. Steeles did that. He toasted the Steele legacy. Money, power, not love. Never love. People used love against you.

Cheyenne thought he'd used her. If necessary, he would,

but not for protection from Stephanie. He could ward off the Stephanies of the world. He hadn't been able to resist the urge to tease Cheyenne. Giving in to temptation wasn't like him.

He could still feel the firm roundness of her hip against his palm. A good reason not to see her again.

"I saw the fish egg lady downstairs. Grandmother said you're gonna marry her."

Thomas looked up. Davy stood in his bedroom doorway fastening his jeans. "Did you wash your hands when you finished?" Thomas asked automatically.

"I will." Davy hesitated. "Is she coming with us tomorrow?"

"No. And I'm not going to marry her."

"Good. Cheyenne is prettier."

"Because she likes peanut butter?"

"'Cuz she smiles a lot." Davy fidgeted.

"What?"

"Do you think my mother smiled at me like Cheyenne does?"

Thomas wanted to ask how the hell he was supposed to know when he'd never met the woman. Instead he asked, "How does Cheyenne smile at you?"

"You know. The fish egg lady looks over my head and smiles kinda like she doesn't feel good. Cheyenne smiles at my face. She likes me." Sidling over to stand by the arm of the sofa, Davy toyed with the snap on his jeans.

"Now what?"

"Do you think my mother liked me?"

Thomas stared in the ruby depths of his wine. How did he answer that question? Davy was as bad as his father. Asking unanswerable questions. Sticking to the truth was the safest. "I didn't know your mother, so I don't know how she felt. But your father..." He cleared his throat of a sudden hoarseness. "David loved your mother and he would have loved you. So I expect your mother loved you, too. Now go wash your hands.''

Halfway across the room, Davy turned. ''Uncle Thomas, you don't smile a lot, but you don't tell me to go away when I ask you something. Is it okay if I like you?''

CHAPTER FOUR

"HE's just another client. The difficult kind. Your cat is on the counter."

"Me thinks my sister protests too darned much. Amber doesn't belong to me," Allie said. "She lives with me."

"Considering you paid the veterinarian's bill when she was abandoned and hit by a car, I think we can say she's now yours."

Allie picked up the yellow, three-legged cat. "What do you think, Amber? Does Cheyenne think she can change the subject when we're talking about a man who's a walking hunk machine?"

"You haven't even seen him."

"Olivia called this morning while you were in the shower. When was the last time you kissed a male client over the age of eight? And in the lobby of St. Chris's."

"I lost a bet to Thomas, that's all."

"Uh-huh. Thomas."

Cheyenne hated it when her sister thought she knew everything. "He's selfish and thoroughly disagreeable."

"Uh-huh."

"Stop saying, 'Uh-huh.' If you want to know the truth, I feel sorry for him."

"Uh-huh." Allie stroked the yellow cat. "And he's a hunk."

"Okay," Cheyenne said, goaded into agreement. "He's a hunk. If you like that type. I don't."

"Maybe he's my type."

"He's not."

"How do you know? You only met him yesterday. He might have hidden charms."

63

"Believe me, he doesn't."

"Olivia mentioned he returned carrying the clothes he wore when he left."

"Olivia must have spent the whole day snooping. I told you he fell in the river."

"Fell in rushing to rescue his nephew."

"He regretted it soon enough. You should have seen the look on his face when he realized I'd saved his fly rod. It was obvious he'd rather have strangled me with it than thank me."

"You can't hold that against him. There's a long line of people who have wanted to strangle you at one time or another."

"If you want to believe Thomas Steele is wonderful, go ahead. I don't have time to argue," Cheyenne said. "I'll admit he's drop-dead gorgeous, his smile is devastating and his gray eyes take on a kind of smoky-green cast when he—" She shoved a piece of toast in her mouth. Darn her runaway tongue.

Allie looked interested. "When he what?"

"Flirts," Cheyenne mumbled around the toast.

Allie set Amber on the floor. "I'm looking forward to meeting Mr. Steele."

He ought to have his head examined. Standing in the middle of the lobby holding gaily-wrapped packages when he should be discussing with McCall new ways of marketing the St. Christopher.

"Mr. Steele?"

She'd butchered her hair. Chopped off the tousled curls practically at her scalp. The short cut completely altered her appearance. Even her eyes looked bluer.

She wasn't Cheyenne. Thomas had never before seen the blond woman crossing the lobby. Cheyenne's height, build, hair color...not her eyes. Cheyenne exposed her every thought and emotion. This woman fenced hers off. "I'm

Thomas Steele. I didn't realize Cheyenne had a twin sister.''

"In twenty years I'll hate you for adding a year to my age. Allie Lassiter.'' She started to extend her hand, then noticed his package-laden arms. "I hope I haven't kept you waiting.''

"You're here exactly when Cheyenne said.''

"I wouldn't dare not be.'' She led the way outside. "When Cheyenne plans something, woe to him who throws sand in the gears.''

"If you're warning me she's the managing type, you're too late,'' Thomas said dryly.

She opened the back of her sport-utility vehicle. "You don't look like the type who rolls over and plays dead.''

"What do I look like?'' He set the packages in the vehicle.

She slammed the back shut. "Cheyenne says you're selfish and disagreeable.''

He was tired of being told he didn't measure up to Cheyenne Lassiter's standards. "How do you women run a successful business when you're so damned outspoken?''

"Do you recommend being dishonest with clients?''

He waved off the bellman and opened the driver's door for her. "I recommend remembering the customer is always right.''

"I thought your nephew was our customer. Cheyenne says he's adorable.'' Giving him an airy wave, Allie Lassiter sped away from the curb. A dog Thomas hadn't noticed hung its long head out the front passenger window and stared back.

Thomas walked slowly into the hotel. It wasn't too late to back out of this excursion with Davy and Cheyenne and the Olivia woman. He must be getting soft in the head to let Davy's question influence him. The boy had probably caught wind of his belated birthday celebration and was angling for more gifts.

The pathetic thing was, Davy's ploy had worked. Thomas had taken care of the shopping list Cheyenne faxed him. And added an item here and there. What did a woman know about little boys? If Thomas was going to be part of this ridiculous charade of a party, he intended to do it right. He could spare one day. Tomorrow Cheyenne and Davy were on their own.

"I can't decide if it's a blessing or a curse the way those girls pick up strays." The elderly lady sitting in a pale green club chair in the lobby looked straight at Thomas.

"I beg your pardon?"

"You heard me. Wait until you're my age to act deaf. People'll believe you and say all kinds of things thinking you can't hear them. Olivia Kent. You don't remember me."

He should have recognized the old harridan immediately. Fifteen years ago he'd been working the front desk in the Chicago hotel and Mrs. Kent had ripped out his guts because he'd ignored her while he flirted with a pretty girl who worked at the hotel. "I was surprised you didn't say something to my grandmother."

"You learned your lesson. I've kept up with your career. Your grandmother Virginia would be proud of you. Henry Jr. doesn't amount to much."

"Henry Jr. happens to be my father," Thomas said stiffly.

"That doesn't make him any more competent."

"My father is president of the company."

"Figurehead. Everyone knows you run things. Henry Jr. might have amounted to something, I doubt it, but your mother ruined him. At least she didn't ruin you. I hear we're celebrating the birthday today of a new generation of Steeles."

"Yes." This woman would make a point of knowing everyone else's business. He seemed to remember her husband had made a killing in oil back in the fifties.

"Celebrating it late." Her faded blue eyes appraised him. "Cheyenne's too good for you, but don't make the mistake of marrying a woman like your mother."

Thomas couldn't decide whether to be amused or offended. Was it Aspen's high altitude and thin air that made people speak so frankly? "I have no intention of marrying anyone."

"What about the hotels? The Steele legacy?"

"You answered that yourself. There's already a new generation of Steeles. Davy." He saw the doorman signal. "Cheyenne and my nephew have arrived. Let me help you to her car." He might kick the old lady's walker out from under her.

Cheyenne stood on the sidewalk laughing with a bellman. Her jeans were too small, and Thomas would swear he saw underwear through the worn patches in back.

Davy wore faded jeans and a battered straw cowboy hat. "I'm a cowboy, Uncle Thomas. Cheyenne and me went shopping."

"Where'd you shop? The city dump?"

"An old clothes place. Cheyenne said new jeans'll rub your skin off when you're riding a horse. C'mon, hurry up, let's go."

"Mind your manners, young man," Thomas said and immediately heard the echoes of his maternal grandmother's voice. The smile slid from Davy's face.

Cheyenne gave him a dirty look. "Olivia, this rip-roaring cowpoke is Thomas's nephew, Davy. I assume you've already had the privilege of meeting Thomas."

Her tone of voice made it clear she didn't consider meeting Thomas a privilege. Davy edged away from him. Wonderful. Thomas had set a new speed record in achieving unpopularity.

Olivia arranged matters to suit her. "Your help, Thomas," she said, beckoning imperiously. "I'm sitting in front. I don't subscribe to the notion that men belong there by virtue of their physical makeup. Davy, you may put my walker in back. Thank you.''

Thomas sat behind Cheyenne and watched her in the mirror, knowing his scrutiny irritated her. Irritation ran both ways. He didn't like being called selfish and disagreeable. "You don't look like your sister. She's a pretty hot number.''

She gave him a cool look in the mirror. "I wouldn't know.''

"She has the right combination of sophistication and sex appeal. She said you're older.''

"One year.''

"That's all? Maybe it's her hairdo. Sexy as hell.'' He had to swallow a laugh as Cheyenne curled her lip. "The kind I see on the streets of New York.''

"In my day, men preferred long hair.''

"Really,'' Thomas said politely. Old biddy. Did she really think Cheyenne Lassiter needed help?

"Thomas hates my hair. He doesn't like bleached, frizzy hair.''

"I like your hair,'' Davy said, "'cept when you hug me and it makes my nose itch. But it smells good,'' he added quickly.

"Thank you, Davy. Just for that, I won't tease you about being a tenderfoot.''

"What's a tenderfoot?''

Thomas quit listening as Cheyenne launched into an explanation which led to a discussion of riding horses. The highway paralleled the Roaring Fork River, and he envied the fishermen in the river, unencumbered by a self-righteous female, a tiresome nephew and a rude old lady.

Cheyenne pointed out Mt. Sopris to Davy and Olivia and then they turned off the highway, heading away from the river, and up into the hills. Sunflowers and some kind of light purple wildflowers grew along the roadside beside the bushes. A bird with blue feathers flew from a tall weed stalk. Some cows stood drinking in the middle of a small creek.

A plume of dust approached from the other side of a hill. A rusty pickup crested the hill and sped toward them. The driver, a man about Thomas's age, waved at Cheyenne. The saintly Worth?

Cheyenne turned in beneath a huge log arch with what looked like two touching circles burned into it. Beneath the arch, swinging on two short lengths of chain, hung an old, painted sign. Thomas scowled at the faded blue words.

"Welcome to Hope Valley," Olivia read aloud. "That sign thrills me every time I pass under it and think about your great-great-grandmother arriving here." Olivia turned toward the back seat. "Cheyenne's ancestors have a great deal in common with your Steele ancestors. They had dreams and worked hard to make them come true."

Thomas failed to see a common bond. Steeles didn't dream. "I'd like to hear about them."

Cheyenne gave him a mocking look in the mirror. "You wouldn't, but I'm going to tell you. My great-great-grandmother left her family back east to come to Colorado by wagon. Years later she told my grandpa, her grandson, she knew they'd be killed by Indians or outlaws, or the weather, or an accident, but she came because she loved her husband. She said she took one look at the valley my great-great-grandfather had claimed, saw a bluebird, wild roses, and a deer drinking from the stream and, for the first time since leaving home, felt hopeful they could make it. Her husband laughed at her for wanting to name the ranch Hope Ranch, so she wrote Hope Valley on a broken board and nailed it to a tree, and we've called this Hope Valley ever since."

He should have known she'd be the gooey, sentimental type.

A minute later Cheyenne braked in front of an old-fashioned, two-story white frame house.

A cowboy walked from a corral by the barn. Thomas deduced from the wide smile on Cheyenne's face as she waved that this was Worth of the so-called gorgeous blue eyes. A cowboy hat shaded the upper half of the cowboy's face, but doubtlessly his insolent swagger appealed to some women. Feeling at a disadvantage in the back seat of the car, Thomas stepped out.

The cowboy looked Cheyenne up and down. As if he owned her. "One of these days you're going to bust right out of those skintight jeans." His gaze took in Davy who'd jumped from the car, checked at the sight of Thomas, then moved on to Olivia in the car. "Olivia," he said in a deep, pleasant voice. "Good to see you again."

"Worth, you handsome devil. Come give me a hug."

Thomas left them to their mutual admiration society while he retrieved Olivia's walker from the back of the car. Davy, his face rapt with awe, stared up at the cowboy, then shifted his legs, imitating the easy stance of the man. Cheyenne locked her arm in the cowboy's. They'd forgotten Thomas even existed.

Except for the cowboy who watched Thomas's every move from the corners of his eyes.

Thomas carried Olivia's walker to the passenger side.

"She won't need that," the cowboy said. He smiled down at Olivia. "And I don't want any lip from you, Olivia. You'll wear yourself out walking across the barnyard. Greeley dug Yancy's wheelchair out of the barn and fixed it up good as new. Here she comes with it."

Two women came from the house. The man had a damned harem.

A blond woman, the same height and shape as Cheyenne and Allie—another sister?—gave Cheyenne a squeeze as she joined them. "Olivia, I'm so glad you could come. You must be Davy." She shook the boy's hand before turning to Thomas. "Welcome to the Double Nickel, Mr. Steele. I hope I can call you Thomas. I'm Mary Lassiter, Cheyenne's mother.''

Thomas hoped his jaw hadn't dropped too obviously. He took the hand she extended. "You can't be Cheyenne's mother." She didn't look a day over thirty. Only close inspection revealed the network of lines fanning out from her eyes.

Mary Lassiter chuckled. "Words to warm an old gal's heart. Greeley, let Worth help Olivia and you come meet Thomas." She drew the slight, shorter woman forward. "This is my youngest daughter, Greeley."

Greeley Lassiter had Cheyenne's mouth and cheekbones, but her face was thinner, and long brown hair hung straight down her back. Thomas would never have guessed she was sister to Cheyenne and Allie. Her cool smile and stiff greeting said she read his thoughts. She didn't offer to shake hands, but he couldn't help noticing her fingers ended in short-clipped nails. Scraped skin decorated several of her knuckles. Catching him looking, she slid her hands into her pockets and turned away.

"Greeley's our resident mechanic," her mother said proudly. "Worth hates machines. I'm convinced an evil genie switched parts of their DNA at birth."

Thomas liked Mary Lassiter. He wondered how such a pleasant woman had given birth to three irksome daughters. "Thank you for having Davy and me. He could hardly sleep last night, he was so excited."

"It's our pleasure. Worth and I get sick of each other's company." She swiveled in response to a question from Greeley.

The cowboy must be her foreman. Thomas covertly studied the man rocking back on his heels, hands tucked in his back pockets, as he talked to the others. Not talked—pontificated. The women hung on his every word. His pose was as phony as he was.

He was shorter than Thomas by at least half an inch.

After some discussion, Cheyenne pushed Olivia in the wheelchair toward a corral where Allie waited with saddled horses and a couple of dogs. Davy skipped happily along conversing with Mary Lassiter. Greeley divided her attention between the pair with the wheelchair and Davy.

If the others had forgotten Thomas existed, the cowboy hadn't. He stood in front of Cheyenne's car watching the parade across the barnyard, but Thomas could feel, not exactly hostility, but more a withholding of judgment, emanating from the other man. His behavior reminded Thomas of two executives sizing one another up before deciding if they could conduct business together.

Thomas decided to take the bull by the horns. Mocking himself for thinking in a country cliché after only a few minutes in a barnyard, he stepped toward the cowboy and held out his hand. "Thomas Steele. We weren't introduced in all the confusion."

The cowboy shook his hand firmly. "Worth Lassiter. Glad you came along. Cheyenne thought you wouldn't."

"Cheyenne thinks a lot of things, most based on her version of life, rather than on reality," Thomas said, conveniently ignoring he almost hadn't come. The cowboy's words belatedly hit him. "Lassiter? You're related to the rest of them?"

"Yeah, lucky me. If Beau had to keep sticking me with his brats, the least he could have done was have boys."

"You're Cheyenne's brother?"

"She didn't tell you? That's Cheyenne. Too busy setting the rest of the world straight to let people in on what's going on." Amusement tinged the sideways glance Lassiter gave Thomas. "We ought to feel sorry for you, but we're just glad you're her latest victim instead of one of us."

"I got her number from the start. Don't worry about me."

"I'm not." The amusement disappeared. "When a man

has three sisters, it takes too much energy to worry about every passing stranger who comes sniffing around them.''

The drawling voice sounded pleasant enough, but Thomas knew a warning when he heard it. He was, in swift succession, astonished, appalled and annoyed. "I hired your sister to entertain my nephew. I have no other interest in her.''

Lassiter studied him for a long moment, then shrugged. ''I should have considered the source. Allie reads animals like an open book, but she's dyslexic when it comes to reading people.''

"Your sister told you I'm interested in Cheyenne?'' Thomas asked incredulously. "I met Allie this morning for the first time and only for about six seconds.''

"You don't have sisters, do you, Steele? It takes them a whole lot less than six seconds to make up their minds, and you can't change their minds for love nor money. Cheyenne's the worst of the bunch. Takes after Yancy when it comes to deciding right from wrong.''

"They're right and everyone else is wrong?''

Lassiter laughed. "In a nutshell.''

Thomas strolled beside Lassiter toward the cluster of people and animals at the corral. "Who's Yancy? Your brother?''

"No, you've met us all. Yancy Nichols was my grandfather. Mom's dad. His grandfather, Jacob Nichols, started the Double Nickel back in the late 1800's. Yancy was pretty rigid about what a person ought to do. Heaven help anyone who disagreed.''

"Such as your father?''

"Yancy didn't waste his time on a lost cause.'' He paused. "That's the big difference between him and Cheyenne. She doesn't know when to give up.''

"My own fishing boots,'' Davy said reverently. "And a fishing vest. Gosh, Uncle Thomas, a fishing pole just like yours.''

"Not quite like mine. You don't need a bamboo fly rod if you're going to use marshmallows to catch fish.''

Leave it to a man to buy the most ridiculous gifts, Cheyenne thought. Davy would outgrow the waders by next summer. She had faxed Thomas a list of possible gifts commensurate with Davy's age and had suggested he buy five or six of the items. Her gaze swept the mound of books and toys beside Davy and she mentally shook her head. Thomas had bought like a kid let loose in a candy store with a fistful of money.

"Open another one,'' Thomas urged Davy who was playing with his new fishing equipment, "or we'll never get to eat.''

"He's more excited than Davy,'' Allie said in Cheyenne's ear. "You'd think he'd never seen the kid open a present before.''

Cheyenne gave her sister a startled look. "I don't think he has,'' she said slowly. It was obvious, now she thought about it. Certainly nothing else she knew about Thomas explained his behavior. When Davy had started opening gifts, Thomas had stood across the room watching. Soon he'd moved to sit on the sofa near Davy. Now he sat on the floor beside his nephew. It was obvious Thomas could hardly keep from tearing into the packages himself.

Davy looked inside the last box, an enormous one, and his eyes grew large. "A train.''

"I used to want one like this.'' Thomas started pulling parts from the box. "It goes around in circles and has a great whistle. And these lights flash red or green, and this arm goes up. It's a train signal. We have to put these tracks together, and then couple these cars...''

Cheyenne fled to the kitchen with her mother and sisters. When she returned with plates for the cake, Worth and

Thomas lay on their stomachs on the floor playing with the train. "Where's Davy?"

"Bathroom," Thomas mumbled. "I think this connects here, and then this one here."

Cheyenne went after napkins. When she came back, Davy was still gone and Worth was asking Thomas how long he'd be in Aspen.

"Less than two weeks. You have the caboose over there?"

"Here. To be honest, Steele, I'll be glad when you leave. Cheyenne cares too much about things. She gets hurt."

Cheyenne stopped short. Of all times for Worth to go into his big brother act. Embarrassed, she backed quietly away. The conversation followed her into the hall.

"She's a big girl," Thomas said. "Where does this sign go?"

"She's a Lassiter. Lassiters worry about Lassiters."

"Look, Lassiter, family loyalty is one thing, but I'm sick and tired of you Lassiters targeting me as the bad guy. How many times do I have to tell you? I'm not interested in Cheyenne. I don't even like her."

Cheyenne hung up the house phone in the lobby. Davy had answered the phone. She hadn't talked to Thomas. And didn't want to. Not after overhearing his words to Worth yesterday. Thomas Steele couldn't possibly dislike her more than she disliked him. At least she didn't shout it to the whole world. If there were any justice in this world, Denver Mint would have dusted Thomas Steele's arrogant backside. Unfortunately, Thomas had easily handled the large, well-muscled bay gelding.

"Disappointed?"

He must have been hiding behind one of the metal columns, waiting to spring out at her. Disappointed that he'd refused to ride the Silver Queen gondola up the mountain today with her and Davy? "No. Where's Davy? He said he was ready."

"I disagreed with his version of ready. Last night I gave him a list of things he needed to do to get ready, and he thought he could slide past a few. Don't frown at me. He's old enough to be responsible for himself. I want to talk to you." He took her arm and guided her across the lobby. Sunlight coming through the atrium's stained-glass dome splashed rose and green on white marble squares. "You hoped I'd fall off the horse."

"I wouldn't be in business long if I didn't do all I could to ensure my client's safety."

"You neglected to ask if I could ride."

"A couple of turns around the pasture isn't riding." What did he want to talk about that he couldn't have said yesterday on the way back to the hotel? A sinking feeling told her this little talk had to do with Worth's warning.

Thomas unlocked the door to The Green Room and waited for Cheyenne to precede him into the lounge, then closed and locked the door behind them. "Davy had the time of his life. He'll talk about that pony—what was his name? Slots?—and his birthday cake and the party and the ranch for months."

"Talk to whom? The housekeeping staff at the hotel?"

"Your brother said you inherited narrow-minded self-righteousness from your grandfather."

"I'm not self-righteous, and he didn't say that."

"That's what he meant. He also warned me off you."

Cheyenne sat on the old-fashioned upholstered piano stool and lifted up the piano keyboard cover. "I can't imagine why he'd do that." She ran her fingers lightly up a scale.

Thomas leaned an elbow on the pale mossy-green grand piano. "I wondered myself. He said Allie told him." His hand came down over hers. His other hand captured her chin, forcing her to look up at him. "Why does Allie think there's something between you and me?"

"I have no idea. I insisted there wasn't."

"Why?"

"Because I don't like you or your attitude."

"I meant, why did you find it necessary to insist?"

"Olivia saw that stupid kiss in the lobby and told Allie. If Worth warned you off, it's your fault."

"I never told you you had to kiss me if you lost the bet."

Maybe he hadn't exactly said the words out loud. "Your intentions were perfectly clear."

"You said double or nothing for yesterday. You owe me two kisses."

"We didn't bet on anything." She jerked her chin free.

"Because you chickened out. You intended to bet me I couldn't stay on the horse, didn't you?"

"No." She ran her free hand over the piano keys, trying desperately to come up with a believable bet.

"You changed your mind when you realized I could ride. What gave me away?"

She hit a discordant array of keys as she looked up indignantly. "You were setting me up? You wanted me to bet you'd fall off, didn't you?"

"I knew I'd win." He drew her up from the piano seat. "I did win."

"You didn't win anything." He stood too close. "We didn't bet." Tension built up beneath her skin. She didn't want to talk about kissing. "Where did a city boy learn to ride?"

"Summer camp when I was a kid. I learned a lot of things there. How to ride, tie knots, build fires, make my bed, swear." A teasing smile crawled across his face. "How to kiss girls."

Cheyenne leaned quickly back, lost her balance, and sat

abruptly on the keyboard. Jarring sound blared through the room.

Thomas leaned over her, his hands on the piano, one on either side of her, penning her in. "There was a girls' camp on the other side of the lake. Naturally the boys snuck over there at every opportunity."

"Naturally." She didn't want to push him away. Touching him could be dangerous. "Move before I break the piano." The piano dug into her back. The keys bit her bare legs. Both discomforts paled beside the unwelcome warmth from his body. A warmth she wanted wrapped around her.

"What about those two kisses you owe me?" One-handedly he untied the scarf knotted around her hair.

She couldn't want to kiss him. Not Thomas Steele. She'd always laughed at physical attraction. Chemistry was for laboratories. Smart women were attracted to a man's personality. Not his broad shoulders. She looked past the shoulders she suddenly, more than anything, wanted to run her hands over. "We didn't bet." She had to talk about something else. Make noise. Drown out the sound of her breathing. "I've always liked this room. I love the stained-glass windows with the pink lilies and twining greenery. I'm glad someone replaced the broken ones."

"Davy's right." He tucked a curl behind her ear. "Your hair smells good."

"The matching painted tabletops were an inspiration. It's interesting that the original owner decided to do the hotel in Art Nouveau. Not what one expects from a grizzled prospector, but maybe he wasn't grizzled. That's such a stereotype. I remember reading he'd seen a picture of the Eiffel Tower shortly after it was built for that Paris exhibition and decided nothing but the latest style for him. I don't think he ever got over coming to America in that miserable steerage. Once he hit it rich—" A hand across her lips cut off her babbling.

"Your mouth drives me crazy every time I look at it."

Her gaze flew to his face. "Don't look at it," she mumbled against his palm. And she wouldn't look at his. Wouldn't think how it would feel to press her lips against his.

He moved his hand to brush fingers along her cheekbone. "A milestone in our relationship. We agree on something."

"What?" She couldn't think with him touching her.

"That I shouldn't look at your mouth." Cradling her face in his hands, he trailed his thumbs over her cheekbones. "So I'll quit looking." He dipped his head.

She had time for one panicky breath before his mouth closed over hers. Heat poured into her body. She gripped the lapels of his suit coat. The silky fabric excited the sensitive skin of her palms. She wanted to rub her palms all over him. Feel his face, his hair, the back of his neck. She wanted to cool her palms against his icy white starched cotton shirt. His mouth felt good against hers. Right. Warm. Soft. Hard. The subtle scent of his aftershave curled enticingly around her.

He broke off the kiss.

She wanted him to kiss her again. She wanted to disappear between the piano keys.

Saying nothing, he lifted her from her perch on the keyboard. She felt his eyes studying her face and prayed he couldn't guess how much his kiss had affected her. Turning, she softly played a simple tune on the piano. "That wasn't fair. You were just guessing I was going to bet you couldn't stay on the horse." She hit an off note. "I'm not going to kiss you again. I don't owe you two kisses."

"You do and you know it, but I'll settle for dinner tonight in place of the second kiss."

His cool voice told her the kiss meant nothing to him. She quit playing and folded her hands together, striving to regain her composure. "I'm not buying you dinner. We didn't bet."

"I'll pick up the tab. We'll eat here at The Gilded Lily. I'm leaving my nephew in your hands for most of two weeks. I want to know what I'm paying for. Bring a detailed plan for entertaining him so I can check it over."

The kiss might not have happened. He could have been kissing the piano for all the impact she'd made on him. He probably kissed women as often as she brushed her teeth. If she had his wealth of experience, his kiss wouldn't have affected her, either. Discussing business at dinner was fine with her. She wanted her clients involved in the decision process. "We'll have to have to eat early. Davy will be starving after our hike."

Thomas shook his head. "Just you and me. I'll see Davy gets dinner. He likes the burgers and chocolate shakes in Café Sullivan, the hotel coffee shop."

He knew something about Davy. Cheyenne considered that progress. She wanted him to realize he and his nephew needed each other. That's all she wanted from Thomas Steele. She certainly didn't want his kisses.

He'd kissed Cheyenne Lassiter to prove a point. For some stupid reason the woman intrigued him. He'd told himself once he kissed her and proved she was a woman like any other woman, he'd be immune. Once he kissed her and proved he could have her if he wanted her, he would no longer want her.

He scowled at the Grade-A idiot in the mirror. The only thing kissing her proved was that he wanted to make love to her on the piano. It had taken every bit of his self-control to pull away from her. He still wanted her.

Wanting her was not an option. Taking her to bed might be a voyage of discovery worth making, but he suspected a woman like Cheyenne considered sharing a bed as a proposal of marriage. He had no intention of marrying her or any other woman.

Grandmother Steele had warned him more than once never to give an opponent an advantage. Seeing Cheyenne Lassiter on her turf showed her at her best, giving her an advantage.

Therefore, his spur-of-the-moment decision to invite her to dinner. A masterful solution. Get her off her turf and on his.

Thomas congratulated himself again as he inserted simple gold cuff links. If he'd brought evening clothes, he'd have worn them. The poor girl probably didn't own clothes suitable for dining at one of the most exclusive restaurants in town. He ought to be ashamed of himself. He wasn't. He was doing her a favor. Tonight, on his turf, she'd look gauche and out of place. Less desirable.

"Gosh, you're all dressed up. Is Cheyenne gonna look like that, too?"

Thomas watched in the mirror as his nephew bounced on Thomas's bed. Bouncing on beds was definitely prohibited. Thomas gave himself a reminder to discuss the rules tomorrow at breakfast. "I assume she'll dress like a girl."

"In a dress? Cheyenne isn't like girls. She's cool."

"I bow to your expertise."

"Does that mean you like her, too?" Before Thomas had to answer, Davy added, "I'll bet she don't have a dress."

I'm counting on it, Thomas thought. "Someone's knocking at the door. Must be your baby-sitter."

"I don't need a baby-sitter."

"Take that up with Cheyenne. She made the arrangements," he said to his nephew's back.

One last inspection in the mirror, a snowy white handkerchief for his pocket, and Thomas prepared to go.

Allie stood in the sitting room of the suite, removing the leashes from two greyhounds. "Hi. Don't you look smart."

"She brought Moonie and this is Chuck's Angel."

"Maybe the St. Christopher Hotel ought to rethink its policy on allowing pets," Thomas said dryly, eyeing the two dogs.

"You'd lose customers. Too many hotels in Aspen allow them, including the Hotel Jerome," Allie pointed out.

"I saw the gray dog yesterday, but where did this lady come from?" He allowed the dog to sniff his fingers.

"She needs a home, Uncle Thomas. Could we—"

"What would your grandmother say if you returned with a dog?"

Davy's face fell. "She wouldn't like it."

"I didn't bring her to persuade you to adopt her," Allie said. "I'm keeping her for a few days until she has a new home. She arrived today, and she's still nervous and confused so I didn't want to leave her alone. Cheyenne tends to be a little narrow-minded when one of these guys destroys our place."

The first sensible thing he'd heard about Cheyenne. "Where is your sister? We have an appointment for dinner."

"She'll meet you downstairs. An old friend waylaid her."

Cheyenne wasn't in the lobby. Or in the dining room. Or in The Green Room. Not that he expected to see her there. This morning he'd realized Ms. Lassiter had her own battles to fight with sexual attraction. After tonight, when they proved so incompatible, they could both rest easy.

Allie said Cheyenne was here. He looked toward Belly's. Thomas P. Sullivan had named the bar "Belly's Bar" for "Belly" Smith, the fat miner who'd sold Sullivan the silver claim which ultimately made Sullivan rich beyond his wildest dreams. Inevitably the bar became known as Belly's. A disgusting name, but Thomas couldn't change it in the face of almost one hundred years of tradition.

Cheyenne was not in Belly's. He didn't think the bar

with its red-flocked wallpaper and prints of half-dressed women would be her kind of place.

Thomas started to walk out when he saw the back of the blond woman standing at the original, hand-carved bar from France. Her low-cut, thigh-high black dress hugged the small amount of body it covered. Long, shapely, nylon-clad legs ended in shoes consisting of a few black straps and ridiculously high stiletto heels. Neon pink toes could be seen through her hosiery.

No woman's skin could possibly be as silky and smooth as her creamy back looked. An earring glittered from her visible earlobe. Much longer and it would touch her shoulders. Her hair had been securely fastened at the back of her head in a fat braid. Thomas couldn't see her face, but he didn't have to.

He knew trouble when he saw it.

McCall must know about the blonde by now. This would be an opportunity to see how the hotel manager dealt with a crisis.

Thomas had no trouble putting a name to the man who possessively held the woman's waist. Last week Thomas had attended the premier of the Hollywood star's latest movie, a movie sure to increase the actor's net worth by ten million or so. Apparently he was celebrating his latest success. The actor had stayed in Steele hotels before, and Thomas knew him casually. He also knew the wife the actor was supposedly so devoted to. If Thomas's memory served him correctly, and it usually did, the actor's wife had dark brown hair and stood a little over five feet tall. This woman towered over the seated actor. One hand rested on the man's shoulder.

The actor caught sight of Thomas in the doorway. "Steele," he called. "Come say hello."

The blonde turned. "Thomas, there you are. I was beginning to think Allie forgot to tell you where I was."

CHAPTER FIVE

HER plan had worked. From the moment he'd spotted her in St. Chris's bar, Thomas had regretted inviting her to dinner. He'd said a few pleasantries to Jake, if one could call words spoken in such a cool manner, pleasant, and ushered Cheyenne into The Gilded Lily without so much as brushing a finger against her. He'd dispensed with drinks before dinner without asking her preference, read the menu with the concentration of one attempting to commit it to memory, and once he'd given their orders, slouched back in his chair and stared around the room, tapping his fingers on the table.

Her plan was definitely a success.

Thomas Steele didn't want to be interested in her any more than she wanted to be interested in him, but it was easy enough to figure out why he thought he was. She was different from his usual women. Cheyenne had encountered the same attitude at college. People had acted as if she were a strange, exotic species because she'd been raised on a ranch out west.

His tapping fingers irritated her.

Now that he'd seen her looking no different from any of a hundred women in New York, he was wondering why he'd kissed her. Good. She wanted Thomas to care about his nephew, not her.

A man who couldn't see beyond a woman's outer wrappings held no interest for her.

How would he like it if all she saw were his outer wrappings? If she looked at him and thought only about how sexy a white shirt could be. Boiled shirts, her grandfather used to call them when he wore them to church. Thomas's shirt didn't make Cheyenne think of church. Neither did the dark suit which made him look taller and broadened his shoulders. A business suit had never before stuck her as clothing which enhanced masculinity. Not that Thomas's needed enhancing. Which he must know, based on his staid, wine-colored tie. A boring tie.

She wondered if it felt as silky as it looked. If he loosened it a little, he might not look so stiff and uptight.

He could quit tapping his fingers. Tapping because he was bored. She was no longer a novelty.

Being proven correct always made one feel smug.

"If you don't stop tapping those fingers, I'm going to break them." Great. Just what the sophisticated Stephanie would have said.

He barely glanced at her. "This is a business dinner, not a date."

"What's that supposed to mean? That you always bang on the table when you discuss business?" She opened her small purse and yanked out some papers. "Here's the schedule you requested. Weather and Davy's interests may call for changes. I'll fax you the night before if I plan something else."

He set the papers down without looking at them. "I expect my business associates to show up at the scheduled time. Not to booze it up in the bar."

"You're mad about that? I told Allie to tell you I'd run into a friend and would meet you down here."

"I'm not mad and Allie didn't tell me you were in the bar with Jake Norton."

"You make it sound as if I were slugging down whiskeys."

"I didn't know you knew him."

"You mean you're surprised I know him."

"If I'm surprised, it's at you fawning over a married man because he's a famous movie star."

"I wasn't fawning. We're friends. He and Kristy stayed

with us when he made the Western film which won him his Academy Award several years ago. They filmed on the ranch, and Jake thought living there put him more into his role. It was uncanny the way he started talking and walking like Worth.''

"Is that why you wore that dress? For Jake Norton?"

She flapped her eyelashes at him. "I wore it for you." Thomas Steele absolutely froze in his chair. Cheyenne would have laughed if the look of horror which flashed across his face wasn't so darned insulting. "Did you think I'd show up in worn blue jeans and embarrass the owner of the hotel?"

"I wouldn't have been embarrassed." He hesitated. "You look very nice."

The compliment came so begrudgingly Cheyenne wondered why he bothered to make it. "I can clean up well, you know. But of course, you didn't know. Which is the point. You think I'm different from the other women you know."

"You are different."

"You only think I'm different, and that's why you think you're physically attracted to me. But, as you can see for yourself, I'm like all the other women you know."

He gave her an arrested stare. "You think dressing like that will stop me from wanting to take you to bed?"

Her heart rate quadrupled and heat rose to her face. "Nobody said anything about bed. I have no intention of sleeping with you."

"Nor do I plan to sleep with you, which is why I proposed keeping our relationship on a business level. I dressed to meet a business associate. I'm not wearing something designed to attract everyone's attention."

"You're certainly not. I don't believe I've ever seen a more boring tie." So boring every woman in the dining room could hardly keep her eyes off him from the minute he'd walked in. The men didn't stare, but their gazes continually wandered in his direction. Thomas Steele didn't need clothes to attract everyone's attention. His sheer presence did that.

The waiter provided a distraction, setting salads in front of them. Cheyenne studied Thomas from under lowered lashes. She couldn't figure out what made him tick. He hid himself from prying eyes, walled himself off from seemingly everyone, including Davy, and yet, when Thomas forgot himself, warmth and humor danced in his eyes.

Emotion scared him.

The conclusion came from nowhere, stunning her with its simplicity. Someone, sometime, had taught Thomas Steele it was dangerous to care. Until she discovered who and why, she couldn't make him care for Davy.

"My tie isn't boring," Thomas said, taking exception to her earlier remark. "It's practical. I don't have time to decide if a tie goes with this shirt or that suit. Everything matches."

She shook her head in mock despair. "I'll bet you don't even own an aqua polka-dot tie or a purple pop art tie."

"That would be a safe bet."

"Have you ever done anything impulsive in your life?"

"I plan ahead and consider all possible consequences. People who aren't willing to take the trouble to plan like to brag they're impulsive. They're not. They're lazy."

"Life happens. You can't plan everything."

"That's an easy way of refusing to accept responsibility."

Cheyenne could see he believed every ridiculous word he uttered. She tried another path. "Olivia told me a little about your family."

"Olivia thinks she knows everything." He added smoothly, "She told me you're too good for me."

"I am not responsible for how Olivia's mind works." Doggedly Cheyenne pursued her goal of learning more about him. "She said your grandparents started from nothing and built the Steele hotel chain through hard work and tons of sacrifice.''

''They did.''

''She also said they forgot how to play and have fun.''

''Buying old hotels and turning them into Steele hotels was their idea of fun.''

''Is it fun for you, Thomas?''

''It's what I was trained to do. Fun doesn't enter into it.''

''Was Davy's father trained to run the hotels, too?''

Thomas carefully drew a small piece of chicken through his raspberry salad dressing. ''Everyone thought he'd want to be in the family business.''

''Didn't he? Is that why you became estranged?''

The waiter removed their salad plates saving Thomas from having to answer. When the waiter left, Cheyenne said slowly, ''I thought your brother was scratched from the family bible because he married a maid. Are you saying he was scratched because he didn't want to run hotels?''

Thomas's eyes darkened. ''He scratched himself. Left a note saying he didn't want to be contacted. Said his wife was his only family from then on. I respected his wishes.''

Cheyenne studied him as the waiter set their dinners before them. Thomas's face gave nothing away. She looked down at her grilled trout. ''Greeley tried that once. The night after she graduated from high school. Said she didn't belong on the ranch. Left a note thanking Mom, and took off. We all went after her. Worth found her at the train station in Glenwood Springs. He dragged her kicking and screaming back to the ranch and told her if she ever treated her mother like that again he'd use his belt on her backside.''

''And she stayed because he threatened her? Was I supposed to go after my brother and beat him up?''

''Worth has never laid a hand on man or beast,'' Cheyenne said indignantly. ''Greeley knew he'd never hurt her. It was what he said when he was so mad he wasn't bothering to be polite. He said what he thought about her hurting her mother. Not his mother or my mother. Her mother.'' At Thomas's confused look, she explained, "Beau met up with a woman in a bar in Greeley. Nine months later the woman showed up with a baby in her arms. Said the kid was Beau's and she didn't want her, so Mom took her.''

"Just like that?''

"Greeley was a Lassiter. I know now there was paperwork and trips to lawyers and to court, but then, I was four and Allie was three, and we thought for the longest time that's how people got babies. Somebody brought them to the door. We never thought of Greeley as half Lassiter and half whatever the woman who gave birth to her was. That's what Worth was telling Greeley. No matter how she came to be, she was Mom's daughter and our sister.'' Cheyenne toyed with her dinner. "We weren't going to let her walk out on us. She's family.''

"If you're trying to compare my family with yours, the situations have nothing in common. How is your meal?''

"Delicious.'' She knew a slamming door when she heard it. "Did Davy tell you about the golden-mantled ground squirrels we saw up on the mountain today?''

"All Davy can talk about is riding your pony. He said you're going riding again tomorrow. Is Olivia going?''

"She left for home this morning.'' Cheyenne smiled. "One ride was all she wanted.''

"I'm curious about that. Didn't you say Olivia was over eighty?''

"Eighty-three. She comes to Aspen with her daughter and son-in-law and books us so they don't feel guilty doing things without her. We've been escorting Olivia around for several years. She loves the ranch, but it wasn't until last year that she told us riding a horse was a lifelong dream of hers. Allie and I put our heads together, and Allie thought we could bring it off. Copper is a placid mare, and Allie worked with her all spring so she wouldn't mind an awkward rider. We weren't sure Olivia would have the strength to hold on, but Worth said he'd ride with her and keep her from falling. I'm glad we could make her dream come true. Olivia was so happy.''

"Is that why you're in the type of tour business you're in? To make dreams come true?'' The mockery in his voice came through loud and clear.

Cheyenne swallowed her defensive retort. A sophisticated woman wouldn't worry about people's dreams. "I'm in it for the money. I used to teach—no money in that. Now I do the tour thing all year. It's really my baby, because Allie still teaches, but she works with me summers and holidays. A number of agencies do Western rides or nature trips or take children or people with special needs, but a lot of people fall between the cracks. That's where I come in. Specialized, personalized tours. People are willing to pay a lot for my services. Like you, I run a niche business.''

"Hotels aren't a niche business.''

"Steele hotels are. A person can get a bed and clean bathroom almost anywhere. Steele hotels provide atmosphere, ambience, history. Not to mention luxury and sinfully lavish care and personal attention. Olivia isn't alone in refusing to stay anywhere else if she's in a city with a Steele hotel.''

"Maybe I'll use you in our next advertising campaign.''

She smiled. "Sweeping through the lobby, dragging a fur coat?''

"I was thinking more along the lines of riding your horse into the lobby, and none of the employees blinking an eye.''

Cheyenne refused to let her smile slip as she mentally kicked herself. The whole point of the hair, the dress, the makeup had been to convince Thomas she was no different from the other women he knew. Women too sophisticated to rhapsodize over his hotels.

Noticing a U.S. senator in the far corner of the dining room, Cheyenne turned the conversation toward politics. From there they discussed art, the theater, food, and finally sports. She kept her comments superficial and impersonal.

It was a relief when she could finally push away her coffee cup. "Thank you for dinner." She nodded at the papers. "Hopefully you'll find Davy's schedule satisfactory, but if you have questions, you can fax me."

"I'll call the hotel limo to take you home."

"That's not necessary. It's a lovely evening. I'll walk back with Allie. We share a condo."

"Then I'll walk you both home."

"It's not far and perfectly safe. There will be plenty of people out, and we'll have the dogs. You can't leave Davy."

Thomas pulled out her chair. "He'll be asleep. Someone from housekeeping can stay with him for a few minutes."

She couldn't help grinning. "You don't know much about little boys, do you?"

He followed her from the dining room. "I used to be one."

She doubted that. "And you went to bed when you had two dogs visiting you?"

"My mother doesn't allow pets in her residences."

They stopped in front of the elevator. "It's good for children to have pets," Cheyenne said.

He pushed the button. "You're going to say a pet teaches responsibility. I learned it without a dog and so will Davy."

"Actually, I was going to say having a pet teaches children to think about others."

Thomas thought about others. Especially one other. Not that he wanted to. He should have realized Cheyenne would sabotage his scheme. Damned woman even bragged about her cleverness. Of all the stupid notions for her to come up with. No wonder she drove her family crazy. Always thought she knew best, Worth said. She could have given Thomas a little credit instead of thinking he wanted her because she'd been raised on a ranch and didn't look like the average female New Yorker.

"Gosh, Cheyenne looked funny last night. Like somebody on TV. I didn't know she could look like that. Why she'd wanna look like a girl?"

Thomas looked up from his breakfast. "She is a girl. A woman."

"She smelled and my nose itched."

Thomas managed not to laugh. "I suppose you thought the dogs smelled better."

"Well," Davy said seriously, "they smelled like dogs. Cheyenne didn't smell like her. She smelled like those other ladies, like the fish egg lady." He frowned. "Do girls think us guys like that smell?"

"Some guys do."

"I don't. Do you?"

Thomas drank some coffee before reluctantly admitting. "I thought she smelled good."

"I think she stinked."

"Keep it to yourself or you'll hurt her feelings."

"Her heart already hurts."

Thomas stopped eating. Did Davy know something about a failed love affair or something about Cheyenne's health? "How do you know?" He was really asking what Davy knew.

Davy obligingly told him. "Allie said Cheyenne's heart is too big and it hurts her. I hope it don't hurt today." He jumped up from his chair. "I'm done. We're going to the ranch. I get to ride Slots. Cheyenne said he likes boys."

"Do everything on your list. That includes brushing your teeth."

Thomas pushed aside his plate and poured himself more

coffee. He had no trouble interpreting Allie's remark about her sister's heart. Not for one second last night had he believed Cheyenne's claim to be in business for the money. The woman was a cross between a bleeding heart and a crusader who'd targeted him to be Davy's surrogate father. Too bad. He'd charted the course of his life, and Davy had no place in it.

Neither did Cheyenne Lassiter.

Which made her invasion of his mind all the more annoying. It was bad enough she haunted his dreams. No surprise there. The woman was a walking sex object with those long legs and that mass of blond hair. She'd make any man hot. That postage stamp of a dress she'd worn last night hadn't helped.

Thomas considered the situation with detachment. He'd always prided himself on being more interested in a woman's mind than her body. He didn't give a damn about Cheyenne Lassiter's mind. He'd fallen prey to pure and simple lust. There was no dressing it up under false pretenses. He wanted to bed her. Period. She could check her mind and her self-righteous viewpoints at the bedroom door. Three seconds of listening to her expound on the way the world ought to be would drive him mad. He slowly set down his coffee. Yes, it would.

He'd discarded his previous plan too quickly. Davy said she'd been like someone on TV. An actress playing a part. Pretending to be sophisticated and knowledgeable. Pretending she belonged in his world. She didn't. The answer was to replace the images in his brain with images of her totally, awkwardly out of place in his world.

Easy enough to find the invitation. He hadn't intended to go, but to send the usual contribution. The party would be perfect. The cause was for animals or something. The invitation had suggested a donation of five hundred dollars per person. Beautiful people. Entrée to an outlandishly expensive house. The cream of the social crop flying in for the occasion. No woman would think of refusing to accompany him to the party.

She'd stick out like a sore thumb. He ought to feel sorry for her. He didn't.

He hadn't asked her to respond to his nephew's stupid advertisement. He hadn't asked her to stir up his life. To stir up his hormones. He hadn't asked her to do anything—except keep Davy out of his hair. A simple enough request. Thomas took one last swallow of coffee and told himself there was no way traces of her perfume from last night lingered in the room.

Every breath she inhaled brought her the scent of her own perfume. And the heady scent of the aloof man sitting at her side on the leather seat. She'd almost said no when he'd phoned her this morning inviting her to join him tonight. Remembering the way he'd laughed last night when Davy and the dogs had managed to drench themselves in the Hyman Avenue Mall fountain, she'd said yes. When she'd first met Thomas Steele he would have ordered his nephew out of the pulsating waters in a forbidding voice. Cheyenne chose to see his laughter as a sign of softening. She wasn't giving up on Thomas Steele yet.

"It's a beautiful evening. The first star is already up. The stars seem closer here," she said.

"They look brighter because they're not competing with city lights."

She knew that. She was merely making conversation, not easy when she sat royally in the back of a limo while someone she knew chauffeured her. "I don't know if it was Davy or Mom who was happier about him spending the night on the ranch." That topic went nowhere. She tried again. "Davy did very well today. He's good with animals. Doesn't rush them."

"He's afraid of them."

"He's cautious. Nothing wrong with that." His body

language told her he disagreed. "Davy takes his time, looks the situation over, and plans accordingly. I'd say that was a Steele trait." Encouraged by a slight grunt of reluctant laughter, she said, "He helped saddle Slots and he mounted and dismounted by himself and afterward, he helped rub Slots down."

"What kind of name is Slots for a pony?"

"The kind you use when your great-great-grandfather, Jacob Nichols, names the ranch the Double Nickel after him and his wife Anna. Jacob took their last name and spelled Nickel like the coin so he could use two round circles as their brand. Then he named his horses after money. His son started using numbers, my grandfather added gambling, well, you get the idea."

"Thus we have Denver Mint and Casino, the horse you rode."

"And Bullion, Sawbuck, Payroll, Sterling, Ten Spot and so on. It's a family tradition."

The limousine rolled to a smooth stop in front of a spectacular sprawling brick and stone house. Floodlights bathed the circular driveway and entrance. Their driver opened Thomas's door, then hurried around the rear of the car to open Cheyenne's door, winking at her as she exited the car.

Thomas spoke a few muttered words to the driver, then lightly grasped Cheyenne's elbow. "I see we're not the first."

"Nor the last." She indicated the line of cars entering the drive. "A good crowd. Allie will be happy."

"Allie?"

"This is one of her pet charities." Thomas's silence spoke for him as they stepped into the cavernous marble-lined foyer. "You don't have a clue what charity this is for, do you?"

"Of course I do."

"Thomas, what a surprise." In the glass-fronted great

room, Stephanie Winston glided up and presented a porcelain profile.

Thomas kissed her cheek. "Stephanie. You remember Cheyenne."

"The cowboy's daughter." She turned toward Cheyenne with an artificial smile, then her jaw dropped as she took in Cheyenne's appearance.

"Nice to see you again." Cheyenne couldn't decide if she was flattered or insulted by the other woman's shock.

"Cheyenne, it's perfect for you. I knew it the minute I saw it." A petite, sable-haired beauty arrived at Cheyenne's side and gave her a big hug. "Jake said red's not your color. Men. It's not red, it's watermelon pink." Releasing Cheyenne, the woman extended her hand toward Thomas. "Hi, Thomas, you probably don't remember me. I'm Kristy Norton. We met at—"

"Of course, I remember you, Mrs. Norton."

"Kristy. Fair's fair. I called you Thomas." She slipped one hand through Cheyenne's elbow and the other through Thomas's and turned a beguiling smile on Stephanie. "You'll excuse me if I take these two away, won't you?" Without waiting for Stephanie to answer, Kristy dragged them across the enormous room and into a book-lined library.

Cheyenne gave a small gurgle of laughter. "I thought you told me you'd turned over a new leaf."

Kristy laughed with her. "Jake's right. It doesn't pay to be nice to hangers-on. They never get the picture."

"I don't think she's exactly a hanger-on," Cheyenne said.

"Whatever. I saw the way she looked at Thomas. You don't hear him complaining, do you? And why should he? I thought Allie looked terrific tonight, but you are dynamite. Isn't she just the sexiest thing at this party?" she demanded of Thomas.

"How am I supposed to answer that when it's asked by a beautiful woman?"

"Handsome and dangerously smooth," Kristy said. "Jake," she said to her approaching spouse, "take Thomas to get a drink. I want to gossip with Cheyenne. We'll have champagne," she called as the men walked away. "Drinks are in the wine cellar. We have plenty of time for you to tell all."

Cheyenne shook her head at Kristy. "You're outrageous."

"Never mind me. What's this about you and gorgeous Thomas Steele? When Jake told me last night, it was all he could do to keep me from running over to the St. Christopher to see for myself. Do you know his reputation? Just about every unattached woman on the east coast—and a few attached ones—would do anything to get him in her bed, but he never plays. How did you do it?"

"He's not in my bed. He's a client."

"Thomas Steele needs a specialized tour guide?"

"Not Thomas. His seven-year-old nephew."

Kristy frowned, then said, "That's right. I did hear something about David leaving a child."

Cheyenne had forgotten Kristy lived in New York City before she married Jake. "Did you know Thomas's brother?"

"Every halfway pretty girl in New York knew him. Then one day he disappeared from the party scene. There were rumors he'd found a new girlfriend, but no one knew who she was. We thought his parents had succeeded in hooking him up with some rich girl. He complained about that all the time, that he and Thomas needed to marry somebody rich."

"Why would a Steele need a rich bride?"

"Daddy Steele made a lot of bad investments."

"But I recently read they plan to acquire a small, deluxe hotel near Central Park in New York City."

"That's now. I'm talking about nine or ten years ago. The only thing that kept the Steele hotels out of bankruptcy court was Daddy Steele turning the management reins over to Thomas. I didn't pay much attention at the time. David's marriage was more interesting."

"You knew his wife?"

"Knew of, like everyone else in New York. It was the scandal of the society page. A Steele eloping with one of the housekeeping staff. I never saw David again, and I felt bad when I heard about the plane crash. All of us girls liked David. He was like our younger brother. We felt protective of him."

"Protective of a Steele? You've got to be kidding. Did you feel protective of Thomas, too?"

"I never met Thomas until Jake and I started staying in Steele hotels. I get the feeling Thomas doesn't have much use for parties. I thought Merrilu was going to faint when he called and said he was coming tonight." Kristy gave Cheyenne a speculative look. "And bringing a guest."

Over Kristy's shoulder, Cheyenne saw Thomas and Jake approaching. "Thomas came because it's a good cause, isn't that right, Thomas?"

"According to your sister." Thomas handed her a flute of champagne.

Jake laughed. "Allie got a hold of us and strong-armed us into—how did she put it, Steele? Increasing our generosity? I want to know how much she got out of Worth."

"Let's go ask him," Kristy said. "I think he needs rescuing."

"Worth?" Cheyenne swung around. Her brother stood listening politely as Stephanie Winston talked, her hand on his arm.

"Who's he talking to?" Jake asked.

"I don't know," Kristy said, "but she's had so many face-lifts, it's a wonder her ears don't meet in the back of her head."

"Kristy, she's a friend of Thomas's," Cheyenne said.

"Oops, sorry, Thomas. Too much champagne, I guess." Her face pink, she buried her face in her glass.

"Champagne, my... Didn't you tell her?" Jake asked.

"I haven't had a chance yet, you big goon." Kristy turned luminous eyes toward Cheyenne. "I told Jake if he told you first I'd kill him and then when I saw you, we got off on another subject." Her eyes darted at Thomas. "Anyway—" she raised her glass "—this is sparkling water." She took a deep breath. "I'm pregnant."

Cheyenne thrust her champagne at Thomas and threw her arms around her friend. "Congratulations. I'm so happy for you."

Kristy hugged her back and the conversation degenerated into excited babble. Eventually Kristy tugged Jake off in Worth's direction.

Cheyenne retrieved her champagne and gave Thomas an apologetic smile. "It probably doesn't seem like such a big deal to you, but Jake and Kristy come from large, close-knit families and they've been trying to have a baby for quite a while."

"I'm not against babies. I just don't want one. I don't want kids. Any kids. I don't want a wife. I don't want a family."

The words and the firm voice he'd said them in should have convinced her, but Cheyenne couldn't help thinking he reminded her of a little boy whistling in the dark, pretending he wasn't afraid. She studied his face. "What do you want, Thomas?"

"I want to kiss the sexiest woman in the room, the one in the watermelon pink dress."

Swallowing too much champagne, Cheyenne choked. Thomas Steele wasn't the kind of man who'd kiss a woman in a room full of people.

When she'd recovered, Thomas gave her a half smile.

"Don't worry. I'm not going to kiss you. It was my awkward way of telling you you look very nice tonight."

She pinned a smile on her face. "Thank you." Nice. He'd been teasing her about Kristy calling her sexy. A shared joke. She kept smiling. "You look very nice, too." She didn't add she wanted to kiss the sexiest man in the room.

If she had said it, she wouldn't have been teasing.

CHAPTER SIX

THOMAS leaned his elbows on the deck's wooden railing. As dark as the night sky was, the mountains surrounding the valley loomed blacker. Pinpoints of light, houses, climbed the hillsides. The lights of Aspen clustered at this end of the valley floor, and he picked out the St. Christopher Hotel, the Wheeler Opera House, the Jerome Hotel and a few other of the Victorian mining town's landmarks.

He knew a little of the town's history. In the late 1870s, miners from Leadville had come over Independence Pass searching for ore. They found silver and the town boomed. With the demonetizing of silver, the miners moved on. Ranchers and farmers settled the quiet valley. Then in the late thirties, skiers found Aspen.

Thomas could see the runs carved out on Aspen Mountain. Those long-ago miners and skiers would be amazed if they saw the town and surrounding area now. Tourists flocked to Aspen for the natural beauty and the skiing, for cultural and intellectual pursuits. To rub shoulders with the rich and the famous.

The rich and famous who stayed at hotels like The St. Christopher.

He'd suggested the area to his grandmother after he'd skied here with college friends, but his grandmother had no interest in hotels not located in major cities. Several years ago, he'd remembered Aspen and purchased the St. Christopher, spending too much to bring it up to Steele standards.

Thomas could take or leave the glittering party scene, but he never discounted its appeal to others. He'd sensed the money in Aspen, and research had supported his instincts. The success of the St. Christopher Hotel validated his investment.

Music from a jazz trio, bursts of laughter and snippets of conversation came through open windows. Old Aspen mingled with new. He'd spotted foreign dignitaries, a Saudi prince, a minor member of British nobility, two congressmen, and businessmen who occupied various rungs on the corporate ladder of wealth and power.

One of The St. Christopher Hotel's bellmen moonlighted as a bartender. Another bellman strolled through the rooms as a guest. Since she'd come as Thomas's guest, Cheyenne had given the young man her ticket so he could mingle with the Hollywood stars, two movie directors and a Broadway producer at the party.

Cheyenne had planned all along to attend the party.

Aspen's small size had disrupted his plan. Cheyenne knew everybody. Movie stars, heads of conglomerates, and CEO's were part of her life in Aspen. She played with them and worked with them through her tours.

A minor glitch in his plan.

To get her out of his head, he had to prove she didn't belong, didn't fit in his life.

He slowly straightened. His life wasn't in Aspen. His life was in New York City.

Last night he and Davy had walked with Cheyenne and Allie and the two dogs to the sisters' condo. Cheyenne had insisted on stopping for ice cream cones. This after she and Davy and the dogs had danced around and through the water fountains. He tried to transfer that picture to New York City. It didn't fit.

She wouldn't fit.

He'd invent a reason to take her to New York City. She wouldn't belong, and he'd see, once and for all, how ridiculous a relationship between the two of them would be.

Not that he was considering a relationship. Sleeping with

her, yes, but not a relationship. A trip to the city would cure him of this ridiculous physical attraction he felt for her.

He didn't want to hurt her. Davy liked her. She was wrongheaded, but it wasn't her fault Thomas wasn't cut out to be Davy's father.

She'd get an all-expenses paid trip to New York. And he'd be cured. Winners all around. She should be grateful. He could have seduced her into his bed. Made her promises he had no intention of keeping. Instead he was giving her a treat.

Cheyenne craned her neck to see the New York City skyline before they headed through the Lincoln Tunnel. "I can't believe I let you talk me into coming."

When Thomas told her he had to make a flying trip back to New York because negotiations for the Park Avenue hotel had hit a snag, her first reaction had been disappointment. For no good reason. She wouldn't miss him. Wouldn't even know he was gone.

Then he'd asked her to come along, calling the trip a bonus for her rearranging her schedule to accommodate taking on Davy. Cheyenne considered his invitation for about two seconds before accepting. Not for the marketing opportunities through the Steele head offices as he'd suggested, but for the opportunity to snoop.

Worth had been opposed to her going, but since he tended to think his sisters were still kindergarten age, she'd paid no attention to him. Or to Allie who'd preached caution, as Allie always preached caution when it came to men. Greeley, ever practical, had asked when was the last time anyone successfully stopped Cheyenne once she'd set her mind to do something. Cheyenne's mom said she trusted Thomas. Mary Lassiter planned to have a lot of fun with Davy, and she told Cheyenne to have a good time in New York.

The trip to New York wasn't about a good time. She'd come for answers. Cheyenne wanted to know why Thomas refused to include Davy in his life. Not for the obvious reasons. Not once had Thomas said he didn't believe in single parents; not once had he said Davy needed a mother; not once had he said his mother couldn't bear to have someone else raise Davy. Davy's few remarks about his grandmother indicated the woman didn't give a hoot about her grandson.

After a rushed packing job, both for her and for Davy who was staying at the ranch, they'd left Aspen the next morning. A small commuter plane flew them to Denver where she and Thomas boarded a flight for Newark. A car and driver from the hotel met them at the airport.

Eager to snoop into Davy's and Thomas's background and circumstances, Cheyenne hadn't delved deeply into Thomas's motives for inviting her. Belated doubts crept in about the wisdom of coming. Why had Thomas really asked her? In appreciation as he'd said, or as a buffer against all the predatory women Kristy Norton had mentioned?

She considered and dismissed the possibility he'd brought her to seduce her. If Thomas Steele planned to seduce a woman, he'd make sure the woman knew. Thomas couldn't have made it clearer he had no intentions of falling into bed with Cheyenne. Not that she wanted him to. It wasn't as if his kiss had aroused any curiosity about making love with him.

"Relax. Johnny's a good driver."

Cheyenne turned to see Thomas watching her. Grateful he couldn't read minds, she seized on the neutral topic. "I'm not used to being driven. Do you ever drive?"

"I have a car garaged near where I live. I drive it occasionally. Normally it's more convenient to use a taxi or Johnny and the car." He put his briefcase on his lap. "I want to refresh my memory on a few points before my meetings. If you'll excuse me?''

Cheyenne dutifully turned her head toward the window as they exited the tunnel. She'd forgotten the noise. Taxis honked and sirens wailed. People moved along the sidewalks at breakneck speed. So different from Aspen. Thomas said they'd go to the hotel from the airport and she could freshen up or rest or whatever. She planned on the whatever. As soon as Thomas left for his meetings.

''I hope to be free tomorrow afternoon so I can take you over to our main offices. How do you plan to spend the rest of your time?''

Cheyenne hoped he didn't notice her guilty start. ''This afternoon I might head over to Fifth Avenue. Tomorrow I'll hit the art museums. The Met for sure, and maybe the Whitney, and the Museum of Modern Art.'' She'd fit them in around her investigating. Investigating sounded better than snooping.

''Johnny can drive you.''

''Thanks, but I'll walk. I love to look at the buildings.''

''You've been here before?''

''Not since college.''

The car pulled up in front of a tall, elegant gray stone building with an Art Deco facade, and soon Cheyenne stood in the middle of an exquisite gilt and marble lobby under the most opulent chandelier she'd ever seen. Before she could fully take in the intricate mosaic-tiled floor and stylized murals high on the walls, Thomas had whisked her into a birdcage elevator.

''I've arranged for my room to be prepared for you.''

''Where are you staying?''

If he heard the slight touch of panic in her voice, he ignored it. ''At my place. I seldom use my room here.'' He led her down a mahogany-paneled hall, through heavy double doors, stopping to unlock a single door. His look encompassed the impersonal room. "If you need anything, call the front desk."

"I do need one thing. Where to find Pearl."

"Pearl? What do you need with her?"

"Davy asked me to say hello to her and a few other people."

Thomas shrugged. "Ask Edward, our head concierge. He's worked here forever. Nothing goes on in this place Edward doesn't know about. He'll know where you can find Pearl." He hesitated. "Don't spend all your time delivering Davy's messages."

"I promised him. It won't take me long." She intended to grill every single person on Davy's list about Davy's life. And incidentally find out what she could about why Thomas had a phobia about caring. Not that he didn't care for Davy. The silly man just refused to admit it.

"What's the smirky little smile for?"

"Thinking about Fifth Avenue brings a smile to every woman's face."

Thomas ran his knuckles lightly down the side of her face and smiled. "Don't spend all your money in one place."

The warm highlights in his eyes did strange things to her insides. She wanted to press her face against his hand. She wanted to melt into his body. She did neither. Gathering her scattered wits, she said, "I won't."

Shutting the door behind him, Cheyenne leaned against it and closed her eyes. Physical attraction, she told herself as if it were a kind of mantra. Nothing but chemistry. Thomas Steele was not her type.

Forcing herself to breathe evenly, she reminded herself her purpose in coming to New York was not to daydream about Thomas. She'd come to snoop. For his own good. He and Davy belonged together. If Thomas couldn't see that, then Cheyenne would show him.

After giving Thomas a few minutes' head start, Cheyenne went down to the lobby.

A gray-haired gentleman with regal bearing stood at the concierge desk. Seeing Cheyenne walking in his direction, he gave her a warm smile. "Ms. Lassiter?"

His name tag told her she'd found Edward. "How did you know who I was?"

"Thomas stopped on his way out and asked me to give you a message. He'll meet you in the dining room at seven-thirty."

"All right, but that doesn't tell me how you picked me out."

"Thomas said to look for a beautiful lady with bright, shining eyes."

"Not the Thomas I know," Cheyenne retorted.

Edward laughed. "I saw you come in with Thomas. Ever since Thomas called to say he was bringing a woman with him, we've all been anxious to see you."

Cheyenne reddened. "It's not like that. We're business associates. He's hired me to entertain Davy." Edward gave her a look she had no trouble interpreting. If she was hired to entertain Davy, why was she in New York without him? "He hired my agency, I mean. Davy is with them." The man nodded, as if willing to go along with a pretense. "He's riding horses," Cheyenne added desperately.

The man's whole face lit up. "Davy's riding horses? How 'bout that? He's always wanted to ride in one of the horse-drawn carriages over by Rockefeller Center. Sammy—" Edward signaled a passing bellman "—Davy's riding horses in Aspen." He turned back to Cheyenne. "What else?"

She listed everything they'd done.

"Thomas went fishing?" Edward asked in shock. "We need to talk some more, Ms. Lassiter, but Thomas said you wanted to speak to Pearl. I caught her as she was leaving for the day and sent her up to Thomas's room. You'll be more private there.''

Cheyenne wondered all the way up in the elevator why she needed to be private. Nothing about the matronly woman waiting at the door to Thomas's room gave her the answer.

Inside the room, Pearl clasped her hands together and asked anxiously, ''How's Davy? How's my baby doing? Is he happy out there in Colorado? I told him Thomas wasn't a monster, but his grandmother put the fear in him, telling him if he didn't behave, Thomas would shut him in his room. I knew he wouldn't, but Davy, he's got an imagination.'' The woman stopped to breathe.

''Davy is fine. He's having a great time, hiking, fishing, riding horses and—''

''Davy got to ride a horse? That's fine. He's always liked horses. He likes me reading stories about them to him.''

''You seem to know a lot about Davy.''

Pearl looked directly at Cheyenne. ''I raised that baby. Me and the others.''

''The others?''

''People who work here at the hotel. Edward, some, although he's a little old now for helping with a little one. To hear Edward tell it, he raised Thomas and his brother all by himself.''

''Pearl, Edward said you were on your way home, but I wonder, do you have time to talk?''

The maître d' escorted Cheyenne through the dining room to the table where Thomas sat. ''I'm sorry I'm late,'' she said.

Thomas stood. ''I was early.'' His gaze swept over her. ''You put your time to good use.''

Yes, she had. Not shopping as he meant. ''Thank you.'' The simple white dress had come from her suitcase, not Fifth Avenue.

A waiter silently materialized and poured her a glass of wine. Cheyenne glanced quickly through the gilt-edged menu and made her choices. Closing the menu, she gazed around the room taking in gleaming wood-paneled walls, gold-framed paintings, elegant chandeliers and a ceiling of red chinoiserie painting and elaborate wood molding. Luxurious chairs upholstered in red, green and gold stripes sat around tables clothed in snowy white. On the tables silver candlesticks held creamy candles topped with small crystal-beaded shades. Heavy lead crystal vases each held a single red rose. In an alcove across the room, a man in evening clothes played soft music on a black baby grand piano. Cheyenne turned to tell Thomas she liked the room.

He was frowning at a busboy across the room, The maître d' glanced at Thomas, then sailed across the ocean of lush red carpeting to the busboy's side.

"Took you long enough," Thomas muttered.

"You frown and the maître d' races across the room. What's that about?"

"It's difficult for me to eat here without monitoring things." He gave her an apologetic smile. "We should have eaten elsewhere."

"Did the busboy do something wrong?"

"When he put on the tablecloth, he allowed the table top to show. We don't allow that kind of sloppiness here."

"What difference does it make? The cloth is on, the table looks lovely. Who's going to notice how it went on?"

"I noticed."

"Because you own the place."

"Because I used to bus tables here."

She knew that. She knew he and his brother had worked almost every job in the hotel. "Good experience," his grandmother had been quoted as saying. Cheyenne had talked to a great many people this afternoon. "Edward's very sweet."

"Edward's a Tartar. We all tremble in our boots when he frowns."

"I don't believe—"

"Thomas. Why didn't you tell me you were returning?"

His face expressing surprise, Thomas looked past Cheyenne, then stood. "Mother? What are you doing here? What happened to your cruise of the Greek islands?"

An elegant older woman kissed the air next to Thomas's cheek. "We had to fly home. I don't know why your father booked us on one of the sailing ship cruises instead of on a liner with stabilizers. He knows I suffer from motion illness. It was agonizing. I knew Paris would be a better choice, but you can't tell your father anything."

"If I'd known you'd returned, I would have brought Davy back."

"Your father insisted I rest up. He doesn't think I can manage a rambunctious child, as ill as I've been. I told him I'm fine, and of course, I miss my grandson terribly, but you know how your father worries. We'd cancel our plans for tonight, but we're going to the Murrays and she'd be devastated and you and your friend don't want to spend a quiet evening with your parents." She patted his cheek. "Edward told me you were in here. I'll tell your father you said hello. And, Thomas, next time, it would be nice if you let us know what you're doing. How does it look when I tell people you're in Aspen and you're running around New York?" One last pat and she left.

Her heavy, expensive fragrance hung over the table.

"That was my mother," Thomas said unnecessarily. "I would have introduced you, but she was in a hurry."

"She didn't ask about Davy. What does she think you've done with him?"

"She trusts me to leave him with someone responsible."

Cheyenne was sure of a lot of things, but that wasn't one of them. It had taken her less than a minute to determine Thomas's mother was the most self-centered person she'd

ever met. The hotel employees she'd spoken with today had
implied Mrs. Steele scored pretty low in grandmothering
skills, but Cheyenne wouldn't have believed it if she hadn't
seen Mrs. Steele in action. Mary Lassiter would have
thrown herself on Thomas, hugging and kissing him until
he couldn't breathe, and she would have demanded every
detail of Davy's stay in Aspen.

They'd discussed the hotel dining room, the food, the wine,
the decor in the lobby, the honking on the streets, the flowers by Rockefeller Center and the Gothic-style old G.E.
Building, now known as Tower 570. They'd discussed the
Park Avenue hotel purchase, they'd discussed the severance
package which had caused the hitch necessitating Thomas's
return, and they'd discussed his belief that a company's
current, knowledgeable employees constituted an integral
part of any purchase. They'd discussed Cheyenne's stint as
a teacher, including her discovery that one of her students
was being abused by his stepfather. They'd discussed her
tour agency.

Beyond Cheyenne's one comment and his brief response,
they had not discussed his mother.

Thomas had had no trouble reading Cheyenne's mind.
He'd felt the disapproval humming through her.

The differences between his mother and hers would fill
the Grand Canyon.

He'd been on the right track when he'd invited Cheyenne
to New York. Not because she wouldn't fit into his world.
Because she'd see he didn't belong in hers. Cheyenne had
a knack for fitting in wherever she went. She'd won
Edward's seal of approval, a feat not easily accomplished.
Thomas had no trouble visualizing her conscientiously delivering all Davy's messages. She'd never trivialize a
child's request. He sensed the abused child still weighed
on her conscience, giving him insight into what had sent

her speeding to the St. Christopher Hotel as soon as she'd read Davy's advertisement.

He should have asked Davy if he could do anything for him in New York. The thought had never occurred to Thomas. The thought never would occur to him. He wasn't cut out to be a family man.

He would tell Cheyenne the truth. She'd met his mother. She'd understand.

She'd pity him.

She'd quit trying to meld him and Davy into a family unit.

She'd entertain Davy, but she'd keep as far away from Thomas as she possibly could.

Out of sight, out of mind. Without her presence to remind him, he'd be able to put thoughts of her out of his head. She'd no longer disturb his nights.

He'd tell her tonight. At his place. That's why he'd told Edward he needed Johnny and the car, explaining he wanted to show Cheyenne a little of the city at night. He'd already pointed out the lit-up Empire State Building and the Chrysler Building. They'd moved slowly through the crowds in Times Square and read the gaudy electric signs. They'd passed Rockefeller Center, Radio City Music Hall, the Waldorf Astoria, Grand Central Station, St. Patrick's Cathedral with its giant rose windows glowing from within, and the United Nations building. He'd run out of reasons to procrastinate.

Leaning forward Thomas tapped Johnny on his shoulder, then settled back against the leather seat. Much too soon they turned down the short street where he lived.

Cheyenne gave Thomas a surprised look as Johnny stopped the car, but she went agreeably into his building, smiling at the doorman who greeted them. Her high-heeled shoes rapped across the black and white marble floor of the lobby. She was the first woman he'd met who could keep up with him without running. She walked with a loose, easy stride. Maybe all Western women walked like that. Strides to fit the countryside.

He shut the door to his apartment and pointed to the undraped windows. "There's a good view of the East River."

She dutifully walked over and gazed out a window.

Thomas switched on the old floor lamp.

She turned her back to the windows and looked around. "I guess you didn't ask me up here to see your etchings."

No pictures hung on the walls. The glass-topped coffee table held nothing but organized stacks of business and industry magazines. Charcoal-colored wool covered sturdy overstuffed furniture from the fifties. His room wouldn't tell her much. Or maybe it would.

"I thought we could talk," Thomas said.

One corner of her mouth turned up. "You mean without everyone in the hotel perking up his or her ears?"

"They wouldn't eavesdrop."

"It wouldn't be eavesdropping. They're interested in what you're doing. You're the big boss."

He failed to see the distinction, but he had more important issues to address. "Would you like something to drink? Coffee? Some cognac?"

"No, thanks, I'm stuffed. I should have skipped the crème brûlée."

He poured cognac for himself. Stalling. Out of character for a man who could stare down anyone across his desk or at the negotiating table.

Those people didn't look at him out of muddy blue eyes which expected the best from him. A best he couldn't give.

He carried his cognac from the kitchen alcove into the living room. She stood at the windows looking out into the night. "Not much traffic on the river," she said.

Polite, meaningless chitchat. Not asking what he wanted to talk about. She must know she wasn't going to like what he had to say. He'd let her enjoy the view for a few minutes before he said it. After she heard him out, she'd agree with him. Putting his glass on the table, he sat on the sofa. "I talked to Davy earlier. He insisted you had to see the 'car building' tonight because he likes it all lit up."

Cheyenne moved to stand behind the wooden rocking chair in the corner. She rested her hands on its back. "He was in the bathtub when I called, but Mom said they're having a great time. She said he gave you all the details."

She didn't sound surprised he'd called. He'd surprised himself. "He rode horses with Allie, rode on the tractor with Greeley, helped your mom bake cookies, but best of all, according to Davy, Worth let him help shovel out the barn." His gut clenched as Cheyenne laughed. He'd miss her uninhibited laughter. Only because he'd always wonder how she'd be in bed.

"Leave it to Worth. One time he suckered Allie and I into sweeping out the barn loft by convincing us he'd read sweeping was a great bust-building exercise."

"You believed him?"

"We were only ten and eleven," she said indignantly. "Grandpa had Worth's liver for lunch when he found out. In addition to his other chores, Worth had to weed Mom's garden the rest of the summer." She made a comic face. "We felt so bad, we helped him with the weeding. Even Greeley helped him."

"Suckering you again."

"He told us we didn't have to, but Worth had pulled us out of so many jams and covered for us so often, we owed him. He makes us so mad sometimes, but he's always there for us." Cheyenne slowly rocked the chair. "You were a big brother, you know how it is."

He ignored her last words. She was guessing. "You're lucky to have a close-knit family."

"I don't know what's so lucky about having three people who know intimately your every flaw and who have ab-

solutely no qualms about pointing them out ad nauseum,"
Cheyenne said darkly.

"Wish you were an only child?"

"Never!" She gave a sheepish grin. "Don't you dare
tell any of them I admitted that. I'd never live it down."

He could put it off no longer. "What's more important
to you? Family or your ranch?"

"Is this some kind of test?" she asked lightly. "Because
it's ridiculously easy. Family, of course."

"If you asked me the same question, hotels or family,
I'd say the hotels were more important."

"You could say it was high noon outside right now, but
that wouldn't make it true."

Thomas should have known she'd be difficult. "You're
the one who pointed out my mother didn't bother to ask
about her only grandchild. Family means little to her. One
of her sisters is married to a wealthy retired senator, so
Mother maintains close ties to her. Mother's other sister
married a sergeant in the air force. Mother sends them a
cheap Christmas card. Other things in her life count for
more than family." He looked fixedly at his cognac on the
table. "I'm the same."

"No, you're not. Was this your Grandmother Steele's?"

Thomas's gaze flew to her. She was running her palm
along the top of the rocker. "Are you listening to me?" he
asked, a sharp edge to his voice.

"Yes. You have a selfish, thoughtless mother. I wonder
why she's the way she is. What were her parents like?"

She was determined to control the conversation. Fine.
Drag it where she would, she couldn't control the ending.
Or the truth. "As youngsters, David and I went with
Mother to visit her mother. Grandmother would say she
was happy to see us, then tell us to go outside and play.
We weren't allowed to touch anything and never offered
anything to drink or eat for fear we'd spill or drop a crumb.

When we got older, she complained because we didn't go see her enough.''

"Luckily you had two grandmothers."

Thomas tapped his glass. "Grandmother Steele lived and breathed the hotels. Granddad, too. It killed him when he was fifty. From then on, Grandmother had time only for hotels."

"She took time to teach you and David everything she knew about the hotel business."

"Because she cared about the hotels. The Steele legacy. Not because she cared about us."

"That's not true."

"It's true," Thomas said flatly. "Quit trying to put your naive spin on my life. We weren't, we aren't, a TV sitcom family. In my family, we don't love people. We love what they can do for us. I don't do family. I don't do love." He grabbed his cognac, gripping the glass tightly. "It's not in me to love." He refused to look at her. He hated this conversation. Hated pity.

"That's the dumbest thing I've ever heard."

Thomas looked up swiftly. Disgust, not pity, filled her expressive eyes. "That's easy for you to say," he snapped. "You have a family. You know how families operate. I never had one."

"Yes, you did. An unconventional family, but a family all the same."

With her family, he shouldn't have expected her to understand. "An unloving mother who barely acknowledges her children's existence except to yell at them until they became people she can brag about, is more than unconventional."

"I'm talking about your real family," Cheyenne said. "The people in the hotel. Edward and Alice and Johnny and his father and Bernardo and Mame and the rest of them. The ones who taught you your manners and made you behave and gave you treats and took you to ball games and covered for you when you got in trouble. The ones who reported to your grandmother how happy you were or how sad you were.

"Once your grandfather died, I'm sure running the hotels consumed your grandmother. If she hadn't taken over the business, what would have happened to the hotels, to your parents, to you?" Cheyenne set the rocker into motion again. "If she were alive, I think she would have dragged David and his wife home by the scruff of their necks. Your grandmother started out as a maid in a hotel. Your grandfather was a doorman. She wouldn't have held Janie's occupation against her."

Stunned, Thomas stared at her. Where had she learned all this? He searched for something to say. "Who's Janie?"

"Davy's mother."

He inhaled sharply, feeling as if he'd been suckerpunched. "How do you know? I never heard her name."

"I asked Edward. You told me he knows everything that goes on in the hotel. You also told me Davy's mother used to be a maid there. It stood to reason Edward knew her. He said she was a fine person who loved your brother very much."

Thomas stared blindly at her, trying to come to grips with the knowledge she'd acquired in a few short hours. "Edward never said anything to me about her," he finally said.

"You never asked him."

She made it sound so simple. It wasn't. Edward must know. Thomas had been younger then, less able to conceal his thoughts. As he hopefully concealed them now. "What has he told Davy?" Thomas never doubted Cheyenne would know.

"Edward hasn't told Davy anything about Janie because he wasn't sure you'd want him to. I told Edward that was stupid, that of course you'd want Davy to know about his mother."

"Mother won't—" The look on Cheyenne's face cut off his automatic response.

"Your mother has made her choices, Thomas. Wrong choices, hurtful choices. I'd dislike her intensely if I didn't feel so sorry for her. She must be miserably unhappy to shove aside the joy a grandson like Davy could give her, but that's no reason to penalize Davy. Unless of course you resent the fact that, if his parents had lived, Davy would have had the loving parents you and your brother never had."

She treaded too close to dangerous territory. "You have no idea what kind of father David would have made."

"Yes, I do, and so do you. Everyone talks about how loving David was. How much you loved him. How much he loved you."

He wanted her to shut up. She knew nothing. "He walked out on me. Walked away without so much as a farewell wave. Told me to stay out of his life. All he wanted was her."

Cheyenne's eyes never left his face. "Whom do you hate the most, him for leaving or her for stealing him away?"

"He never would have left except for her. It was all about sex. He was sleeping with her. Got her pregnant. They had to get married." He stopped abruptly, horrified by what he'd said. By his lack of control. The snarled words hung in the air. He fought to regain his composure. "I don't hate either one of them. Whoever told you I loved David was wrong. We fought all the time. He was obnoxious and whiny and weak."

"You took care of him, protected him. He adored you."

Thomas laughed harshly. "You're unbelievable. You've turned my life history into some kind of fairy tale because you want me to adopt my nephew. Don't bother to deny it. I've known from the beginning what you had in mind."

"I have no intention of denying it. Davy needs you and you need Davy."

"He doesn't need me." Thomas slammed his glass on the table. Cognac sloshed over the rim. Pulling out his handkerchief, he methodically wiped his hand and dried the tabletop. "Get this in your stupid blond head once and for all. I don't need him."

She walked across the room and perched on the arm of the sofa, her long, shapely, nylon-clad legs almost touching his thigh. "All this furniture belonged to your Grandmother Steele, didn't it? You must have had it recovered."

He hadn't had too much to drink. So it wasn't him. It was her. "You're crazy."

"Maybe." She reached over and ran a finger down his tie. "But I don't think so."

"Then I'm crazy, because I thought you'd run screaming into the night."

She swung her legs around to cross his and slid down the sofa's arm, coming to rest on his lap. "I know you did." She started to loosen his tie. "Every time I see you in a tie, I want to do this."

Thomas grabbed her hands. Her perfume constricted his breathing. "Do what? Take off my tie?"

"Yes." She smiled into his eyes. "And then, I'm going to kiss you."

CHAPTER SEVEN

"Kiss me?" he repeated blankly. "Why?"

Cheyenne almost laughed at the look on his face. She suspected it took a lot to throw Thomas off balance. "Because you're so kissable." Shrugging off his hand, she finished unknotting his tie.

He shook his head as if to clear it. "I'm kissable?"

"Yes." She unbuttoned the top button of his shirt. "I tried to think of some way to subtly encourage you to kiss me tonight, but I'm afraid I'm not too good at subtlety, so I'm telling you straight out. You don't mind, do you?" She liked the warm, hard feel of his thighs under her.

"What if I did?"

Cheyenne concentrated on curling one end of his tie around her finger. "If you're not interested, I won't insist."

"Thank you. I feel better knowing I won't have to fight you off. Or fight your brother because I insulted you by refusing to kiss you."

He'd recovered his equilibrium and had decided to be amused. She gave him a beneath-the-lashes look. "I suppose women want to kiss you all the time." She wanted to scratch those women's eyes out. They couldn't possibly understand Thomas as she did. Whether he admitted it or not. "It's not nice to make fun of me."

"I'm not making fun of you."

"You are. You know very well Worth is more likely to congratulate you on your good sense than fight you if you refuse to kiss me."

Thomas smiled, but said only, "We could continue this discussion in the bedroom."

Cheyenne sat very still and looked him directly in the

eye. "I don't want to mislead you, Thomas. It's not that kind of kiss." The refusal came surprisingly hard.

"I wasn't aware there are categories of kisses."

She knew that. Framing his face with her hands, she said, "You know a lot of things, Thomas, but what you don't know about love and kisses would fill a million encyclopedias."

He stiffened. "Perhaps you'd better tell me what kind of kiss you have in mind," he said levelly. "I won't be bribed into taking Davy on as my responsibility."

"Give me a little credit. I know I don't have what it takes to persuade men into doing something they don't want to do. My brother and sisters have told me often enough that I'm too tall, all arms and legs, have a mop of frizzy, dishwater blond hair and my eyes are the color of bread mold." She smoothed out his wrinkled tie. "And I'm a little bossy."

"You're a lot bossy."

"Never mind that now." She slid his tie back and forth beneath his starched collar. "I like you. I didn't at first, and I never thought I would, but I do. I like how polite you are to your mother despite her behavior, and I like the good things your employees say about you. They idolize you. I'm glad you don't lay off the employees of a hotel you buy and I'm glad you defend your father." She laid a finger across his lips. "Okay, I snooped."

"Why?"

"Davy."

"Did you think you could find something to blackmail me into taking him?"

The question made her smile. "Thomas, if you had secrets which I could use to blackmail you, you'd hardly be the person I'd want caring for Davy."

"I'm not the person you want taking care of Davy."

He didn't get it. "I like the way you talk to Davy instead of down to him. I like the way you bought him a razor and took out the blade so he can shave with you every morning. I like—''

''Grilling my employees is bad enough. Grilling my nephew is unconscionable,'' Thomas said coldly, attempting to shift her from his lap.

Cheyenne locked her hands behind his neck. ''You don't know much about children, Thomas. They love to talk and they love to be listened to. Heaven knows what Davy has said about me.''

After a second Thomas's body relaxed. ''He said you hate peanut butter, but I made you so mad, wild horses couldn't make you tell me.''

''The little snitch. What else?''

''You think I'm the handsomest man you've ever seen and you'd pay a king's ransom to hop into bed with me.''

''I never—'' Her indignation fled before the laughter in his eyes. ''You made that up.''

''It's better than a beautiful woman wanting to kiss me because I treat my nephew decently.''

''I don't want to kiss you because you treat Davy decently.'' She trailed her fingers up his chest. ''I want to kiss you because you're the type of man who treats his nephew decently.''

Thomas exhaled impatiently. ''Then quit babbling and do it.''

''You don't have to shout. I will.'' Her mouth almost touching his, she couldn't stop herself from asking, ''Do you really think I'm beautiful?''

''Yes—'' he grabbed her face and pulled her mouth to his ''—but you talk too much.''

Thomas cradled her face in his hands and molded her mouth to his. Cheyenne's entire body warmed and hummed. An exotic kind of electricity zinged through her, swelling her breasts and tingling deep in her stomach. Pleasure and need mingled until she no longer knew one from the other. She only knew she wanted more. Curving her arms tighter around his neck, she parted her lips, inviting him to deepen the kiss. He tasted of cognac. He tasted male. Thomas male.

She slid her hands beneath his jacket, enjoying the feel of his silky shirt beneath her roaming fingertips. His body heat penetrated the fabric to warm the palms of her hands. His skin would feel silkier. The third button gave her trouble. Grabbing the edges of the shirt, she yanked them apart. Thomas gave a smothered laugh as the recalcitrant button went flying.

Cheyenne spread her fingers wide, loving the heat of him beneath her palms. His heart beat strongly, steadily. She moved her hands, her fingertips lightly grazing the smooth skin stretched tightly over flesh and sinew.

Touching him wasn't enough. Breaking off the kiss, she ignored his muttered protest and pressed her mouth to the middle of his chest. His skin burned her lips.

Suddenly she had an urge to do something she'd never ever had an urge to do. Her mouth closed over Thomas's right nipple. He sucked in air, his fingers clamping down on her shoulders, his thumbs meeting at the base of her throat. His heartbeat speeded up. Or maybe it was her heart thudding in her ears. A spicy odor clung to him, half soap and half male. Her tongue curved over the tiny, hard nipple. Tangy, a little salty. She'd never realized what an aphrodisiac a man's nipple could be.

"Do we get to take turns?" Thomas asked in a slightly thickened voice.

Cheyenne froze as reason returned. Somehow she'd come to be half lying on the sofa. If it weren't for Thomas's arms, she'd tumble to the ground. Carefully she buttoned his shirt. "I'll find the button and sew it on, if you have a needle and thread."

"I don't."

"I'm sorry."

"Forget it," he said impatiently. "I have dozens of shirts."

She gave him a smoldering look. "I wasn't apologizing about that. I wouldn't have ripped it off if the button had come out of the buttonhole, but it wouldn't, which wasn't my fault, so naturally I had to grab it, but—"

He cut off her explanation. "What are you apologizing for?"

"For being selfish. I was so intent on my own pleasure, I didn't think. I'm sorry."

His eyes narrowed. "You're apologizing because you played with my nipple and you won't let me play with yours?"

It sounded worse put into words. "I only meant to kiss you. On the mouth, I mean. I don't know what got into me."

"My nipple for one thing," he snarled.

She knew exactly why he was as testy as a stallion penned away from the mares. "All right." Taking a deep breath, Cheyenne turned her back to him. "Fair's fair. Unzip."

"Just like that."

"But no more than I did."

"You are the world's most infuriating woman." Thomas stood, dumping Cheyenne.

Fortunately she landed on the sofa. Sitting up, she pulled her dress over her legs. It hadn't seemed so short earlier in the evening. "You're mad because you think I'm a tease."

"Let's say I'm confused." Thomas raked his fingers through his hair.

"I wanted to kiss you because I like you and because I heard so many good things about you today. I also wanted to kiss you because I don't think you got your share of kisses while you were growing up. And I admit I enjoyed it when you kissed me the other morning." She pulled down on her skirt again. "That kiss wasn't like this."

Thomas leaned against the wall across the room. "Like what?"

Meaning it hadn't been like anything for him. Cheyenne swallowed hard and forced herself to continue. "Like throwing starter fluid on a barbecue grill that's already burning. You know, whoosh. An incendiary explosion."

"Let me get this straight. You kissed me because you felt sorry for me and got more than you bargained for."

"Yes. Well, no, not about the feeling sorry for you part, because I don't feel sorry for you." She tucked her legs beneath her and pulled a couple of throw pillows over her exposed thighs. "Thank you for letting me, you know, play. It was very nice."

"Very nice," he repeated in a strangled voice.

"I know it didn't do as much for you. That's why I thought I ought to offer to let you..." Her voice trailed off at the glowering look he shot her.

"What it did for me," he said in an ominously quiet voice, "was make me want to rip off every stitch on your body so I can make mad passionate love to you all night long."

It took her a few seconds to control her breathing. "Me, too," she finally said. "Go ahead and say you told me so."

"Am I stupid or are you speaking a foreign language?"

"You told me we had this physical attraction between us, and I didn't take you seriously. You were right." She managed an embarrassed smile. "One kiss and we want to fall into bed."

"I get the feeling that's not going to happen."

She stared fixedly at his left ear. "It's not that I don't want you to rip off my clothes, because I do, and I know how frustrated you must be, but you're the one who's always going on about what a mistake it would be. And you're right. It wouldn't mean anything other than purely physical gratification. Someday, Thomas, you'll find a woman you'll love and you'll have children and you'll be glad we didn't get carried away."

"I'll be glad or you'll be glad?" he asked coolly.

"It may take a while before I'm glad," she admitted. "I never realized how powerful chemistry can be. I mean, why you? There's plenty of sexy-looking cowboys and rich playboys and well-built athletes playing around Aspen. Why do you churn my insides?"

"I don't believe I've had this conversation with another woman."

"I like you, Thomas. I like Davy. I'd like to know how he gets on. I'd like us to keep in contact, to stay friends. Meaningless sex would get in the way of that."

He stared at her for a long moment. "You're trying to spare my feelings, aren't you? Telling little white lies. When did you plan this little charade? At dinner or while we were riding around the city?"

"You think I deliberately seduced you and then refused to go to bed with you? Why would I do that?"

"To spare my feelings."

"You're the one talking a foreign language."

"I told you from the start I can't love. You didn't believe me, until you met my mother. Now you see me as some kind of emotional cripple, and you want nothing to do with me. You want a man who knows how to love. Who is capable of love. What a fertile brain you have to come up with such a complicated plan. Pretend you're dying to ravish me and dying to have me ravish you, only you have to take the high road for my sake. It's a total fabrication. Congratulations. I almost believed you."

No one but Thomas could reach such an incredible conclusion. "Steele is the perfect name for you." Cheyenne could think of only one way to convince him he was wrong. Kicking off her shoes, she jumped to her feet, ignoring the pillows flying every which way. "It's not your heart that's encased in steel, it's your brain.'' She reached for her zipper and yanked on it. "Come help me. My zipper's stuck."

Thomas stood riveted to the wall. "What the hell are you doing?"

How obtuse could a man be? "I'm trying to take off my dress so we can spend the night ravishing each other."

Thomas absently lathered his beard. He'd definitely wanted to take her to bed. Why he hadn't taken Cheyenne Lassiter up on her offer would remain one of the world's unanswered questions. He'd yelled at her to leave her clothes on and phoned Johnny. After waiting endlessly for the car, Thomas had unceremoniously bundled Cheyenne into it and sent her back to the hotel. Alone. Then cursed himself the rest of the night.

He'd arranged for her to visit the office without him, and she'd been subdued on their flight back to Colorado. She hadn't alluded to the previous night. He was damned if he'd mention it. The past two days she'd picked up Davy in the morning and delivered him back at night. If she spoke to Thomas, her conversations were confined to the merest polite commonplaces. The weather. What she and Davy planned to do.

Which was how he wanted it.

A woman like Cheyenne deserved a better man than he.

Finally realizing that, she wasted no time flirting with Thomas, inviting him to join them, messing with his tie.

She said not another word about wanting to kiss him.

Exactly how he wanted it.

Unable to love her, he'd drag her down, take the bounce out of her step. Out of her hair.

She couldn't say he'd ever been less than honest with her.

"Cheyenne tells lies."

Thomas looked in surprise at the seven-year-old face sharing the mirror. He'd have preferred a little dishonesty in New York if that would have propelled her into his bed. "Why do you say that?"

"Allie said. Cheyenne tells lies about people. She says they're good when they're really bad."

Apparently Thomas wasn't the only one to disapprove of Cheyenne's starry-eyed, unrealistic attitude. After thirty-some hours in the bosom of the Lassiter family, Davy would be a gold mine of information. Thomas eyed Davy's innocent face and debated mining his nephew for nuggets of information about Cheyenne. "I don't think Allie meant Cheyenne actually lies."

"Uh-huh. She said Cheyenne lies to herself really bad. How can you lie to yourself, Uncle Thomas?"

Using Davy wasn't playing fair. He'd answer Davy's question in a way which would turn his nephew's attention to something else. "Lots of people lie to themselves. They want something to be a certain way so badly, they lie and say it is that way. Take your father." Mentioning David wasn't so difficult after all. "He wanted a pet so badly, one day he convinced himself if he showed up at the hotel with a puppy, your grandmother would let him keep it." Thomas had been unable to convince him otherwise. Or adequately console David when the inevitable happened.

"Did she let him?"

"No."

"I didn't know my father wanted a dog."

"Every mutt in the neighborhood followed David around." Thomas smiled at the memory. "He was crazy about dogs."

"Me, too. I'm just like him." Davy beamed at his uncle.

"Just like," Thomas said, wiping the suddenly blurry mirror.

Davy concentrated on removing his lather for almost five seconds before asking, "Did you know Cheyenne's father is in Heaven, too?"

"I knew he died. How did you know?"

"Greeley told me." Davy gave Thomas a sideways glance in the mirror. "I told her my father was cool. She said I was lucky. She didn't like her father. She said he was like a—a—one of them fancy cars. Looks good but you can't count on it. Greeley is funny, isn't she?"

Greeley apparently saw her father more clearly than Cheyenne did. "I don't know her very well," Thomas said.

"She's a hugger like Cheyenne and Allie. Mary—that's their mom—she told me to call her Mary. She's the worst hugger. She's always hugging. I asked Worth if all that hugging made him sick, but he said he liked it. I told him you and me don't like hugging. He said that was okay. Some guys like it and some guys don't. He said I could tell them not to hug me, but—" Davy shrugged "—I don't want to make 'em feel bad."

"What made you say I don't like hugging?"

"You and me never hug."

Thomas pressed a warm, damp towel against his face. Hugging didn't run in the Steele family. David hadn't understood that at first. As a little tyke he was always hugging Thomas and wanting to be hugged back. He'd outgrown the habit. Thomas wouldn't admit it to a soul, but in weak moments, he'd missed those hugs. He wondered if David had hugged his wife. What had Cheyenne said her name was? Janie. "Your mother's name was Janie," he said abruptly. "When we get back to New York we'll talk to Edward. He knew your mother. He can tell us about her."

"You think he has a picture? So I can see what she looked like. I'll bet she was pretty. Like Cheyenne."

"I'll bet she was." Very pretty to catch David's eye. Except David had known plenty of pretty girls. Thomas wondered how Janie had attracted his brother. David hadn't come from the usual Steele mold. He'd been kind, generous, impulsive.

A follower. Until he'd met Janie, the person he'd followed most often had been Thomas. Thomas stared into the mirror. David had thought Thomas could do no wrong. If his older brother said a thing was so, it was so. David had come to Thomas for advice on school, on friends, on girls.

He'd never told Thomas about Janie.

Because he knew how Thomas would react.

Thomas would have disapproved of David dating a maid. Thomas had nothing against service people. The most exclusive hotel lived or died, not on its glamour or decor, but according to its level of service. Thomas had the utmost respect for those who cleaned the bathrooms, did the dishes, and made the beds. He'd learned that respect from his Grandmother Steele.

Until Cheyenne told him, Thomas had not known his grandmother been a maid. He didn't question why she'd never told him. He knew. She thought he'd be ashamed of her.

"How come you're looking so funny at yourself, Uncle Thomas? Like you don't like you."

"Sometimes I don't like me."

"I like you," Davy said quickly. "I don't think you're stupid."

Thomas had no trouble figuring out where that came from. "I assume Cheyenne told you I was."

Davy slapped his hand over his mouth. "I'm not supposed to tell," he mumbled. Removing his hand, he added, "She said it just slipped out. Like it slipped out of my mouth. Why did she say it?"

"Why, why, why," Thomas said in mock annoyance. "Why do you ask so many questions?" A knock sounded at the door. "Go answer the door. I think our breakfast has arrived."

Davy dropped his razor in the sink and dashed out of the bathroom ignoring the lather remaining on his face. Thomas absently wiped clean the sink. He'd been honest with Cheyenne about his inability to love, so she thought he was stupid. His only stupidity was expecting her to understand.

He'd be better off being honest with himself. He missed his brother. Not because of some maudlin emotion. Because of ego. Thomas had grown accustomed to David looking at him with eyes filled with hero worship.

Janie had stolen that from Thomas and Thomas resented it. And her.

He carefully folded his and Davy's towels and hung them up. A habit carefully cultivated and enforced by his Grandmother Steele who'd been death on anyone who left a mess for the maids to clean up.

Leaning over the sink, Thomas braced himself on the cold marble and avoided looking in the mirror. He wouldn't like what he saw. A man from whom his grandmother and brother hid the truth. For fear of his reaction.

He'd let them down. More proof he couldn't love. Or be loved.

When you loved someone, you trusted him. His grandmother and his brother hadn't trusted him.

They were right not to.

Cheyenne was wrong. He was not the person to raise Davy. He'd turn him into another Thomas Steele.

He shook his head. This questioning the past, the indulgent self-analysis, was all Cheyenne's fault. Her and her babble about love. The high altitude didn't help. The air was too thin for him. He needed more oxygen. More auto exhaust. And city din. The rigid structure of skyscrapers and the hustle of people busy minding their own business.

He'd let the craziness of Aspen get to him. The free-wheeling, freethinking, free loving.

Love was never free. Love came with a price. He wasn't willing to pay that price.

Even if he could.

A few more days and he'd return to where he belonged.

He wouldn't miss Aspen. He wouldn't miss Cheyenne. He wouldn't miss Davy.

He may as well be brutally honest with himself. If Davy

had grown on him, it was only in Davy's role as David's successor. Someone to look up to Thomas as David had. Hero worship.

Davy was big on hero worship. Cheyenne, Allie, Greeley, Mary Lassiter. Thomas'd had a surfeit of Lassiters and a surfeit of Davy quoting them as if they were some kind of gods. And Worth. Worth was the worst. Telling Davy it was okay if Thomas and Davy didn't like to hug. What business of Worth Lassiter's was it? If Thomas felt like hugging, he'd hug.

Davy hadn't returned. He must have started breakfast without his uncle. Thomas snapped off the bathroom light, passed through his bedroom and stopped short in the doorway to the living room. "Mother."

"Come over here and kiss me hello. I'm too exhausted to move. It's ridiculous we don't have a company jet. A person would think we were poor."

"I'm sorry you're tired. You shouldn't have come," Thomas said, dutifully presenting his cheek.

Davy pushed his spoon back and forth through his oatmeal. He shot a betrayed look at Thomas.

"You're as bad as your father. I always overdo, but I was brought up to do my duty. I can't let poor health stop me."

His mother was healthier than any horse he knew. "What duty brings you to Aspen?"

"You and Davy. I could tell in New York you were annoyed I wasn't well enough to take him off your hands."

"I wasn't annoyed. As you can see, he's fine."

His mother waved a dismissive hand. "It's too much trouble for you to move, but I'm sure there's an available room."

"I'll move. You can stay here."

"Whatever you want. I hate to be a bother. You know me. I can manage anywhere."

Thomas ignored the fiction. "How'd you get here so early in the morning?"

His mother accepted a cup of coffee. "There was a horrible wait last night in Denver between planes. Your father would have had a fit if I'd sat in the airport that long, so I called up Kitty Singleton and she made me spend the night with her. She insisted I charter a plane this morning. I knew you wouldn't like it, but she wouldn't take no for an answer." She made a face. "Kitty's not much of a cook. I probably ought to eat something, but I don't want to interrupt your breakfast."

"Eat my breakfast. I'll eat downstairs in the café."

"I really should have a bite, and then rest awhile."

"You do that. I'll take Davy with me. We won't need to disturb you again."

In the elevator Davy looked at his shoes and made no attempt to beat Thomas to the lobby button.

"Something wrong with your oatmeal this morning?"

"No."

"Want to eat a second breakfast with me?"

The question met with a shrug.

"Want to tell me what's the matter?"

Another shrug.

Thomas felt ridiculously inadequate. He'd thought he and Davy were past the days of poor communication, but Davy had clearly shut him out. Thomas had no idea how to restore the lines of communication.

"She's gonna be mad," Davy muttered to the floor.

"Who's going to be mad?"

"Cheyenne. We was just going to a dumb ghost town and to see some dumb marble you can't even play with, so it don't matter to me. Tomorrow we was gonna ride with Allie's group, but I probably wouldn't get to ride Slots, some dumb kid would, and Slots is dumb anyway, so I don't care, but she'll think I don't wanna go with her."

"Do you want to go?"

"Don't matter."

"I thought you and Cheyenne were having a good time."

"It was okay."

"You mad at her?"

"No."

"Mad at me?"

Davy shook his head without looking up.

"Did Grandmother say something to upset you?"

"How come you told her to come?" The words came in a rush. "She'll spoil everything. She said after I had a nap we'll go shopping. I hate shopping and only babies take naps."

Thomas almost laughed out loud. Focused on handling his mother, he hadn't considered Davy's viewpoint. He dropped a hand on Davy's shoulder as they stepped from the elevator. "I didn't know your grandmother was coming, and her arrival won't change anything. I'll explain you have plans. Grandmother will see someone she knows, and she'll be too busy to worry about us."

Davy looked up hopefully. "I can go with Cheyenne?"

Thomas kept his face solemn. "I hate to force you to go to a stupid ghost town."

Davy grinned from ear to ear. "I don't mind. Honest."

In the café, they ordered breakfast again. Davy kicked at a table leg and gave his uncle uncertain looks.

"Now what?" Thomas asked.

"You won't tell Cheyenne, will you? What I said about Slots being dumb."

"No, I won't tell Cheyenne."

"Tell me what?"

Thomas stood. He couldn't figure out how she lit up a room simply by walking into it. A quick greeting here, a cheery word there, and waiters and guests alike smiled in her wake. The clouds disappeared from Davy's eyes and he sat up straight, his whole body practically bubbling with happiness. No wonder Davy had called her "the happy tour lady.'' She wore a nondescript blue shirt, ordinary jeans and hiking shoes. A dark pink scarf tied her hair at the base of her head in a mass of curls. Nothing about the sunglasses propped on her baseball cap or her muddy blue eyes or the wide-mouthed smile or the face shining with good health indicated she was anything special.

Thomas's body tightened. He wanted that light in her eyes, that exuberance, that interest directed at him. Incredibly, he was jealous of his seven-year-old nephew. He had to get out of Aspen. Get free of her.

''Hey, guys, you gone deaf? Was the question that hard?''

He couldn't remember what she'd asked. Not that he kiss her again. He knew that. He should have taken her to bed. That was his problem. That and being an idiot. Weren't you supposed to feed a fever? She was a fever in his blood. Inexplicably so. It wasn't as if she had experience. Her kiss told him that. Hell, he didn't know why he wanted her. He just did.

''I guess I have to tell her, Uncle Thomas. It was my fault.''

Davy's voice pulled Thomas from unprofitable thoughts. ''Tell her what?''

''What I said. I'm sorry, Cheyenne. I didn't mean to tell Uncle Thomas you said he was stupid.''

Davy gave Thomas a conspiratorial look which Thomas had no trouble interpreting. His nephew had gone with what he felt was the lesser of two evils. Thomas wouldn't give him away.

Cheyenne laughed. ''Don't worry about it, Davy. I shouldn't have said it to you, is what I meant. I don't mind in the least saying it to your uncle.''

Thomas let that one go. He wouldn't mind making her take back her words, but the middle of Café Sullivan wasn't the place. He'd show her stupid. He'd kiss her stupid. Kiss her until those smiling lips smiled a smile of an entirely different nature. One of satisfaction. Lazy satisfaction. She'd look good wearing nothing but a smile of lazy satisfaction.

She raised an eyebrow at him. Damned woman. Thought she could read his mind. "I can't argue with you. I am stupid."

Her brows knit suspiciously, then smoothed. "You want me to ask. I won't. Ready to go, Davy?"

"He has to brush his teeth first. Run ask Mr. McCall where you can brush. Tell him you can't disturb your grandmother." As Davy ran off, Thomas said, "The hotel keeps new toothbrushes on hand in case a guest forgets his." He didn't know why he bothered to explain to Cheyenne. "Sit and have some coffee while you're waiting. Then I can sit and finish my breakfast."

She dropped on a chair. "Your mother is here?"

Thomas resumed his seat. "Showed up unexpectedly this morning. As I told Davy, our deal stands."

"Your mother might have other ideas."

"She'll be relieved to have Davy out of her hair."

"A family trait."

Thomas slowly replaced his coffee cup in its saucer. He didn't know why the obvious solution to his problems hadn't occurred to him before. He quickly analyzed the solution from all angles. Neat, tidy, no loose ends, no downside. The solution to everyone's problem. "As you say," he slowly agreed, his mind on how to lay the proposal before her, "a family trait."

"She's your mother, Thomas, so I shouldn't say this..."

"But you will."

"You have to admit, she's not exactly the perfect grandmother."

"As your mother would be."

"I don't know about perfect, but she'll be great." Cheyenne made a face. "She goes on and on about how she's ready. All she has to do is get us to cooperate and give her grandkids.''

"You could be first.'' Thomas looked directly into her face. "Marry me and Davy could be her grandson.''

CHAPTER EIGHT

HER mouth hung open, but Cheyenne couldn't seem to close it. With difficulty, she pulled herself together. "You should be more careful. What if I'd thought you were serious?"

"I am serious. I'm proposing you and I get married."

He didn't look as if he'd come down with a terminal case of insanity. He didn't look crazy in love, either. "Why?" She didn't know if she was asking why he was asking or why he wanted to marry her or why she should marry him.

"Davy had the answer from the beginning. I need a wife so he can have a mother."

"That's why you're asking me to marry you?" She knew the police chief. Once she explained, he'd completely agree she'd had no choice but to carve Thomas up with a grapefruit spoon.

"Think of it as a business merger. By combining our assets, we'll both come out ahead."

After she carved him up, she'd scatter the pieces from the Copper Queen gondola. He'd make great fertilizer for the wildflowers. "What," she asked in an admirably calm voice, "assets of mine are you interested in?"

He actually had the nerve to leer at her before answering. "Besides the obvious, you'll make Davy a good mother. Living with his grandparents isn't fair to him or them. They've raised one family, and Davy needs younger parents. I run a business. I don't have time to care for him on my own."

"But I could?" He didn't need any more rope to hang

himself, but his inane logic fascinated her in a sick, perverse kind of way.

"You know how to handle kids. You like Davy and he likes you. You'll provide him with a mother, and your family will give him added support and stability."

"I assume Davy and I would live here in Aspen."

"I'd bow to your wishes on that detail. You'll probably want homes in more than one location."

Cheyenne leaned her elbows on the table and rested her chin on her linked hands. "Let me get this straight. Basically, you'd be hiring me on a full-time, permanent basis to take care of Davy. Until when? He goes off to college? Gets married? What happens when you decide he's of an age where he no longer requires my services? A civilized divorce?"

He frowned thoughtfully. "Good questions. I hadn't considered that far ahead. We'll write up a contract which covers all the eventualities. Not the usual prenuptial," he hastened to add. "I know you won't try to cash in on the marriage. I'm thinking in terms of a benefits package. Health care, retirement plan, pension, that sort of thing."

"I see." He actually believed she was considering his asinine proposal. "Am I to understand that this so-called benefits package is the asset you're offering me?"

"One of them."

Cheyenne looked at the coffee the waiter set before her. The stylized floral carpet would not be improved by brown liquid dripping off Thomas Steele's thick head. "What other assets are you offering me?"

"A generous allowance. A home or homes. Suites in any of the Steele hotels. Here, New York City, New Orleans, San Francisco, San Antonio, Charleston, the San Juan Islands. We're negotiating on St. Bart's in the Caribbean, in Victoria, Canada and plans are in the works to expand to Nantucket or the Outer Banks. Naturally your family would be welcome at any Steele hotel any time there's room.''

Her anger faded at his answer. Is that all Thomas thought he had to offer a woman? ''Were you contemplating a merger of me and the Steele hotels or you and me?''

''I am the Steele hotels.''

Not a hint of boasting tinted the matter-of-fact statement. Cheyenne wanted to weep at how Thomas perceived himself. Or howl with laughter at the idiocies he spouted. ''A woman sleeps in a hotel, Thomas. Not with one. I want to know exactly what role you'd be playing in this merger. CEO? Boss? Or husband and father? Did you plan to marry me and go your merry way, thinking of me only when it came time to sign my allowance check? Let's call it my salary. You wouldn't even have to sign the check personally. We could continue as we do now. I could fax you Davy's schedule and you could fax back acceptance or objections. We wouldn't ever have to meet.''

''I'm not hiring you to baby-sit. I want you for my wife.''

''Maybe you ought to spell out exactly what my duties as your wife would entail.''

''This isn't about duty.''

''All right. Function. Expectations. What would you expect from me?''

''You know, the usual.'' For the first time, a hint of discomfort crept into his manner.

''The usual. Ironing your shirts? Fixing meat loaf?''

''You're being deliberately obtuse.''

''You're being deliberately vague. You want me to take care of your nephew and you expect 'the usual.' Would you sign a contract which used such ambiguous terms?''

''All right,'' he ground out, ''I would expect to sleep with you.''

''In the same hotel? In the same room? In the same bed? Sleep how?''

"You know damned good and well I mean I want to have sex with you. And don't pretend you don't know what I mean by that."

"Suppose I said I'd take care of Davy, but I don't want to have sex with you?"

His eyes narrowed. "You won't."

"Will that be in the contract, too?"

"Does it need to be?"

"How often? Once a day, a week, a month? Do I fly to where you are or do you fly to where I am?"

Thomas leaned back in his chair and folded his arms across his chest. "You're not interested," he said flatly. "Why don't you say it outright instead of playing games?"

"Is that how it's done in the world of big business?"

"Being straightforward saves time."

"If you say time is money, I'll fall down on the carpet and throw a screaming fit."

His jaw tensed. "Yes or no?"

He sounded like a belligerent ten-year-old who knew he was in trouble and was pretending he was too tough to care.

Cheyenne wanted to take the ends of Thomas's tie and strangle him. She wanted to take him in her arms and soothe and comfort him and tell him it was okay, that he was okay. Neither would answer.

Standing, she walked around the table. Thomas pushed back his chair and before he could rise, she sat on his lap. "When you ask someone to marry you, you're supposed to kiss her. Even if it is a business merger."

"This isn't the time or place."

"You picked it, not me." Wrapping her arms around his neck, Cheyenne covered his mouth with hers. A split second later, two hard arms locked her to Thomas's body. She loved the taste and feel of him and followed his lead when he deepened the kiss. The muted sounds of the café faded away. Only Thomas existed. Then, reluctantly, Cheyenne broke off their kiss.

Thomas gave her a slow smile. "You won't be sorry."

She wanted to cry, but she managed to return his smile. "No."

"The sooner we get married, the better."

Cheyenne shook her head. "You asked me yes or no. The answer is no."

Angry disbelief turned Thomas's eyes to burnt charcoal. "You're refusing? Turning me down after kissing me like that in a room full of people?"

"Six people. In this kind of hotel guests sleep late or have breakfast in their rooms."

"I don't give a damn where they eat. Why'd you kiss me if you were going to say no?" His eyes narrowed. "Was it some kind of test? To see if I turn you on."

Cheyenne pressed a palm against his cheek. "You know you turn me on."

He shoved aside her hand. "You're crazy. You sit on my lap and kiss me in public. You tell me I turn you on, but you won't marry me. Give me one reason why not. Never mind. I know. Love." He spat out the word like a curse. "You don't love me."

"You're partly right. It's about love. You think you aren't capable of loving. That's not true, Thomas." Quickly she said, "Let me finish. If I marry you, you'll never learn you can love." Her eyes burning, Cheyenne gave him a feeble half smile. "As tempting as all those hotel rooms are, for your sake, I have to say no."

Thomas grabbed her around the waist and raised her to her feet. "I'm not a child to be consoled with vague assurances that it's for my own good."

The word "consoled" almost changed her mind. She clamped her lips together before she could accept his proposal. She knew she was right. If she married him now, he'd never fall in love with her. Maybe he never would anyway. But he might.

He might fall in love with someone else.

Had her mother felt this way about Beau? Loving him, Mary Lassiter gave her husband the freedom he craved. No matter how badly it tore her up inside. Cheyenne thought of all the times she'd seen her mother gaily wave goodbye to Beau and then shut herself in her room. When Mary Lassiter came out of her room several hours later, not one member of her family said a word about her red-rimmed eyes. Once, Greeley had started to say something, but a ferocious look from Worth had silenced her. Then Worth had hugged Greeley hard.

Cheyenne wished Worth were here to hug her now. She wanted to bawl. To tell Thomas she'd marry him. She wanted to run and hide. To throw things. She wanted her mother.

"As far as I'm concerned, our little conversation here never took place," Thomas said abruptly.

As if she could forget it.

He continued curtly, "No reason to say anything to Davy. It has nothing to do with him."

"I thought it had everything to do with him."

Thomas looked over her head. "Here he comes. He'll continue in your care until we leave."

"I'll see he has a memorable time."

Switching his gaze back to her, Thomas said, "Memorable's not the word I'd use." He walked away.

He wasn't talking about Davy.

Cheyenne swiveled about and watched him cross the lobby toward his nephew. Davy ran the last few steps to his uncle, an eager, expectant look on his face.

The same look she undoubtedly wore on her face when she saw Thomas coming toward her.

Logic flew out the window when love entered the picture. A person would take one look at Thomas Steele and Cheyenne Lassiter and know they had nothing in common. That person would be wrong.

Thomas was wrong.

No matter how much he denied it, Thomas cared about people. From caring to love was a tiny step. A tiny, enormously huge step. Love required trust and boldness. Thomas Steele, CEO of the Steele hotels, was renowned in the business world for his farsighted, innovative, aggressive thinking. How funny to know deep inside was a frightened little boy afraid to love. Afraid to trust. His boasting of his inability to love—he could call it honesty all he wanted—was nothing more than a wall he'd built around himself for protection. The woman who could breach that wall would be amply rewarded.

Cheyenne intended to breach that wall.

His proposal of marriage had tempted her almost beyond endurance, but agreeing to Thomas's terms would not only be marrying him under false pretenses, it would cement his doubts and fears. He had to admit he loved her.

He had to love her.

She had no idea when she'd fallen in love with him. Maybe when he'd fallen in the river rushing to rescue Davy. The trip to New York had explained how a man who professed to be cold and unfeeling could behave in warm and caring ways.

Experts debated the relative importance of heredity and environment. Thomas had been graced with the best of both. His Steele grandparents had passed on to him their work ethic and sense of fair dealing. Edward and the others at the various Steele hotels had raised Thomas and his brother with love and affection and caring discipline.

Thomas's mother and father had played such minor roles in his upbringing they barely rated courtesy titles. Unfortunately, the mere act of bringing a child into the world gave parents incredible power to hurt and wound and cripple. Thomas's parents had abused that power. Cheyenne cared nothing about them.

She cared about Thomas.

He had to care about her. He had to.

Thomas gave Davy a farewell pat on the shoulder, and Davy ran toward her.

"Burning daylight," Davy said, quoting Worth quoting one of his favorite John Wayne movie lines.

Meaning it was getting late and they were wasting time.

Getting late. Time running out.

She had to do something to fix this situation. Soon.

"I don't understand why your mother invited mine to the ranch for lunch, or why my mother accepted," Thomas said in an undertone.

Cheyenne followed the direction of his gaze. Ellen Steele dominated the conversation while her mother politely listened. Turning her head, Cheyenne gave Thomas a look of bland innocence. "Mom likes you and Davy. It's natural she'd want to meet your mother." The skepticism on his face deepened. Thomas might be a lot of things, but he wasn't that stupid. He knew darned well who'd engineered the meeting.

A meeting which wasn't living up to Cheyenne's expectations. The idea had seemed a good one. Demonstrate to Ellen Steele the error of her ways so she'd behave more lovingly toward Thomas so he would quit foolishly believing Steeles didn't love.

Cheyenne's family was right. Cheyenne was hopelessly, stupidly naive. Ellen Steele wasn't the kind of woman who'd think another woman was better at anything than her. Soaking up mothering tips over lunch wasn't going to happen.

In Cheyenne's backup scenario, Thomas would see the contrast between their mothers and realize his behavior resembled Mary Lassiter's a whole lot more than it resembled Ellen's. Thomas Steele had more generosity and thoughtfulness in his little finger than his mother did in her entire body.

Not that Ellen Steele would agree with Cheyenne.

Ellen Steele considered herself perfect. "Thomas," she said, her voice carrying down the table, "is exactly like my mother-in-law. She lived and breathed hotels. People didn't exist. David, on the other hand, took after my side of the family. Artistic, interested in everything."

Cheyenne felt Thomas stiffen at her side. She'd screwed up. Thomas's mother criticized him with every other word.

Mary Lassiter smiled warmly at Thomas and said to his mother, "Allie told me you decorated the family suite at St. Chris's."

"An exhausting chore which took me forever to get right, but I've always been one to persevere. My husband says there's no quit in me. I should have done the rest of the hotel. I told Thomas those people didn't know what they were doing. Anyone could see those colors would look dull and dingy."

"They're muted," Thomas said evenly.

"Naturally I'm wrong. According to Thomas I'm always wrong. I don't know why I bother saying anything. Davy, we don't pet a dog at the table. Go wash your hands."

"Cheyenne said your negotiations went well in New York, Thomas," Worth said.

"His father doesn't think so. The employee package Thomas offered is far too generous. I don't know how he reconciles paying them all that money when he's so stingy, he absolutely refuses to allow me to spend a few dollars for a painting for the lobby of our San Antonio hotel."

"More than a few, and I don't think a modern painting by Jackson Pollock fits with the hotel's decorating scheme."

"Naturally, since it was my idea. What do I know? I'm just your mother."

"Speaking of dollars," Allie said, "we raised a lot of money the other night. Before it dribbles away, we need to work out a budget and some short-and long-term goals.

With your financial expertise, Thomas, maybe you have some suggestions.''

"Thomas doesn't believe in charity. I can't drag him to a fund-raiser, no matter how good the cause.''

Cheyenne thought of the program he'd initiated to hire people who needed a helping hand and the college scholarships for employees and their children. She kept her mouth shut.

Greeley related an amusing story about how green with envy some people were when she told them she knew Thomas Steele, the famous hotelier. Cheyenne was sure her sister made up the tale.

Fanciful stories about Thomas continued. Cheyenne could have told her family Thomas didn't need defending, but she let them rally around him, praising him to the skies, droning on about his wonderful talents and qualities.

"I think Thomas is the smartest man I've ever met," Allie said. "Don't you, Cheyenne?''

"Cheyenne thinks he's stupid." Davy had returned.

"You must have misunderstood her," Mary said quickly.

Cheyenne welcomed Davy at her side. Squeezing him affectionately, she said, "No, he didn't. Thomas can be stupid.''

The loud knock on the door came as Cheyenne finished brushing her teeth. A little late for visitors, particularly after a long and busy day. The hotel limo had picked up Thomas and his mother following lunch. Cheyenne and Davy rode horses, then drove back to her place where they'd eaten tacos and watched a rented video before she'd delivered him back to St. Chris's. Allie was spending the night at Hope Valley.

Her visitor had his back to her, but through the small security peephole, she recognized the shoulders. Tightening the sash on her bathrobe, she opened the door. "What are you doing here? Is something wrong with Davy?''

"Wrong question." Thomas stalked into the condo. "The correct question is, would a man prefer people think he's stupid or think he's pathetic?"

"I don't do very well on multiple choice questions."

"The correct answer is 'C.' Neither." He glowered at her from the middle of her living room. "What was the point of that ridiculous charade at lunch?"

She'd expected him to see the amusing side. She hadn't expected anger. "You didn't think it was funny when Greeley said any man who understood the inner workings of an elevator was a born mechanic? Or when Allie went on and on about you riding Denver Mint? She made him sound like a killer horse."

He didn't crack a smile. "You didn't answer my question. Why did you do it?"

"I didn't do anything except suggest to Mom she invite your mother to lunch. Mom loves having people out to the ranch. It wasn't my idea that everyone say all that silly stuff about you. My family sometimes goes overboard when they feel—"

"Sorry for someone?" he interrupted.

"I wasn't going to say that. Your mom kept sliming you and they leaped..." Her explanation faltered at his withering look.

"To defend me. That's what you were going to say, wasn't it?"

"They did it because they like you."

"Heaven help the person your family doesn't like," he said in a nasty tone.

"What a rotten thing to say."

"More or less rotten than what you've said about my mother? Never mind. I accepted long ago what my mother's like, but I don't appreciate other people mocking her."

"No one was mocking her. From what you said about her mother, I'm sure your mom can't help what she's like.

My family acted as they did out of friendship for you. Is that concept so difficult for you to accept?''

"You're the one who has difficulty accepting concepts," Thomas said. "Like the concept of reality."

"I accept reality. That doesn't mean I think things are written in stone. People, situations, can change."

"I'll tell you one situation which is changing. Davy and I no longer require your services."

Cheyenne convulsively clutched her bathrobe to her neck. "Why not?"

"We're returning to New York in the morning."

"You planned to stay three more days." This evening she'd worried three days wouldn't be enough time. Now even those days were being taken from her. He couldn't leave. Not now.

"Situations change." He threw her words back at her.

"What changed?"

"Mother wants to return."

"You and Davy don't have to leave."

"He needs new clothes for school."

"He has a couple of weeks before his school starts." She struggled to decipher what Thomas wasn't saying. "Are you punishing Davy because you're angry about lunch?"

"I'm not punishing Davy. He's better off separated from you."

"Because I told him you were stupid? I apologized for that. I knew I was wrong the minute I said it. You can't blame Davy for repeating it. He's only seven."

"It has nothing to do with that. Today, at lunch, after his grandmother sent him to wash up, when he returned to the dining room, he went straight to you."

"I wasn't trying to compete with your mother, if that's what you think." None of this made sense to her.

"He likes you too much," Thomas said flatly.

Thomas couldn't be jealous. "He likes you, too. In fact,

he's crazy about you. He talks about you all the time and—''

''I don't care about that,'' Thomas said through his teeth. ''He's getting too attached to a passing stranger. The sooner I get him away from you the better. I don't want him to start having ideas.''

''Ideas?'' she asked numbly. How could Thomas call her a passing stranger?

''You know what kind of ideas. Thinking of you as a substitute for his mother. We know that's never going to happen. It's best to make a clean cut. I told him tonight he won't be seeing you again. I said I'd tell you goodbye for him.''

Her throat constricted painfully. ''I thought, I hoped, we could stay in touch. I showed him how to use the fax machine so we could fax each other. I thought you and I...'' She gestured aimlessly.

''Davy will be busy with school.''

''What about next summer?''

''He'll go to camp.''

''And you?'' Cheyenne could barely get the words out. ''Will I be seeing you again?''

''No.'' He walked past her toward the door, adding in a clipped, impersonal voice, ''Send your bill to McCall. He'll see I get it.''

She couldn't believe it. He was walking out, just like that. ''That's it? A few days ago you asked me to marry you.''

''I asked. You said no. The subject is closed. And now any other business between us is concluded.''

''You never cared for me at all?'' How could she have been so wrong? She'd believed what she wanted to believe.

''I cared that you gave good service. I cared that you entertained Davy and kept him out of my hair.''

''That's all I was to you? A baby-sitter?''

"I told you how it was from the beginning. If you chose to ignore my warning, that's your problem."

"No, that wasn't my problem. My problem was I thought you were human," she said, her voice shaking with anger. And hurt. "I thought I'd begun to see the real Thomas Steele. The one hidden beneath the steel exterior, except the steel exterior is the real Thomas Steele, isn't it? You're not a man, you're a machine."

"You saw what you wanted to see," Thomas said coolly.

No, she hadn't. She couldn't have been that wrong about him. He'd built his defensive wall higher and thicker than she'd realized. If she couldn't breach his defenses against her, maybe she could reach him about Davy. She'd survive, but they needed each other. "Thomas, wait." Cheyenne barred his way to the door. "Davy wants desperately to love you. Let him. Love him back. He needs you. You need him."

"I don't want a lecture on raising children." He put his hands on her shoulders to move her aside.

Her hands clamped about his. "I'm not talking just about Davy. I'm talking about you. You can't turn your back on love. It's out there, waiting for you." Love waited for him here, but he was too blind to see it.

"If you want to believe in fairy tales, go ahead. Believe in the Easter bunny and pots of gold at the ends of rainbows. Believe in anything you damn well want to believe in. Just leave me out of it." He thrust off her hands and reached for the knob.

Cheyenne threw herself in front of the door. "I can't. I know there's a human being hidden in there somewhere."

Thomas uttered a short, harsh laugh. "Worth warned me I was your latest victim. Not that I needed warning. From the morning you stormed up to my suite to rescue Davy from a nonexistent situation, it's been clear you think you know better than anyone else how a person ought to live his life. You amused me at first, but the novelty has worn off.''

The brutal words hurt. As he meant them to. ''Don't do this, Thomas. Can't you see what you've been doing? Your parents think of no one but themselves. Everyone said you adored your Steele grandparents, then your grandfather died and your grandmother had to run the hotels. It's not surprising you felt abandoned.''

''No one abandoned me.''

''I know that. You're the one who doesn't believe it. Your grandmother left you her life's work, Thomas. She kept it going for you. David loved you. Everyone says so. He died too soon to tell you. Janie would have loved you.''

''I didn't come to talk about this.''

''Why did you come, Thomas? You could have phoned me, or faxed me, or even had Frank McCall tell me.''

''I don't ask underlings to do my dirty work.''

She hugged her arms. ''I'm just an unpleasant chore?''

''What did you expect? Sentimental sludge about falling passionately in love with you?''

''No, I didn't expect that.'' Hoped, maybe. She squeezed shut her eyelids. Despite her efforts, one tear escaped to slide down her cheek.

''More manipulation? Forget it. My mother's used that trick so often, I'm immune to tears.''

She spread her palms flat against the cold, hard door at her back. ''Will you kiss me goodbye?''

''No. You rejected my kisses when you rejected me.''

''I didn't reject you. Maybe it sounded like I did, but—''

He grabbed her chin, holding her face immobile as he sneered down at her. ''Having second thoughts about turning up your nose at what you'd gain by marrying me?''

''I don't want hotel suites, Thomas.''

''I have nothing else to give you,'' he said harshly. His fingers tightened painfully on her chin and then slowly, as if drawn against his will, he lowered his head and covered her mouth with his.

His body pressed her against the door. She welcomed the pressure, the warmth, the hard, unyielding feel of him. She'd never get enough of his kisses, his mouth, the taste of him. She traced the outlines of his face, memorizing it with her fingertips, even as her mouth memorized the feel of his.

He caressed her cheeks, then slowly slid his fingers down her neck, pausing to draw small circles under her ears with his thumbs. The sounds of his beating heart and her shallow breathing filled her ears. Thomas slipped his hands beneath the collar of her bathrobe. His touch aroused an aching need deep within her. She threw her arms around his middle, holding him close, wanting every inch of her body molded to his.

Thomas broke off the kiss.

Cheyenne's eyes snapped open. She wanted to lock his image in her brain. Steady gray-green eyes, eyes without a hint of emotion, returned her look. She searched in vain for even the tiniest flame of sexual attraction and felt herself shriveling away. Failure. Loss. Mere words. Words filled with incredible pain. She wanted to deny them. She wanted to scream at Thomas. Shake him. Make him love her. Slowly she fumbled for the doorknob behind her. "Goodbye, Thomas. I..." No words which could possibly matter came to her. "Goodbye," she repeated.

He didn't laugh and say it was all a joke. He didn't kiss her again or ask to stay. He walked out. Away from her.

Cheyenne leaned against the closed door for a long second. "Be happy," she whispered. "Find love." Crumpling to the floor in a heap, she wanted to cry. Tears wouldn't come.

Too late, she thought of things she might have done. Words she should have said. If only she'd told Thomas she loved him. She'd given herself any number of reasons for not telling him. They hadn't known each other long enough. Her love was too new and fragile to expose to Thomas's skepticism. Endless rationalization. Lies.

Thomas accused her of refusing to face reality.

Cheyenne faced reality now. Faced what she'd known all along. The truth she'd hidden deep within herself. She was a fraud. Afraid to trust in love.

All her lectures to Thomas about love, and she'd been afraid to tell him she loved him. Afraid history would repeat itself. She'd lost track of the number of times she'd told her father she loved him, and he'd laughed and patted her on the head and walked out the door. He'd never loved her enough to stay.

Thomas hadn't loved her at all.

Amber crept cautiously into the room. The cat stared at Cheyenne from unblinking yellow eyes, then walked over to rub sinuously against Cheyenne. Cheyenne buried her face in the cat's warm side. Amber's fur grew wet with tears.

The ringing phone dragged Cheyenne from a troubled sleep. Every bone in her body ached. She'd fallen asleep on the living room floor in front of the door. Memory returned and the ache spread to her heart. Thomas was leaving.

The phone rang again. Maybe he'd changed his mind. Cheyenne struggled to her feet and dashed across the room.

"Hello," she said hopefully into the receiver.

"Is Davy there?"

She forgot all else at the sharp concern in Thomas's voice.

"What's wrong?"

"He's run away."

CHAPTER NINE

"WHAT do you mean, he's run away?"

"He's run away is what I mean."

"Are you sure? Maybe he went downstairs to breakfast."

"There's an idea," Thomas said with heavy sarcasm. "Why didn't I think to check? Don't be an idiot. I've searched the hotel from top to bottom. I quizzed the entire staff and set them searching everywhere we could think of. A maid and one of the bellmen saw him earlier this morning, but they paid no attention to where he went. He's not here now."

"He loves the fountains on the mall. He could have—"

"That thing he calls his smeller is gone."

"His sniffer. Maybe one of the maids threw it away."

"I asked."

"Your mother?"

"No," he said impatiently. "Davy took it with him."

"You think he'd come here?"

"Where else?"

"To see someone who works at the hotel."

"McCall is phoning everyone who's off."

"Thomas, what exactly did you say to Davy last night?" Cheyenne asked slowly.

"What the hell kind of question is that? I told him we were leaving for New York this morning. I didn't give him a reason. All I said about you is that I'd tell you goodbye for him."

"What did he say?"

"He didn't say anything. He went to bed."

"He didn't ask any questions, like 'why?' when you

155

tucked him in? That's not like Davy. He asks why about everything.'' Silence greeted her remarks. Impatiently, she asked, ''Thomas, you did tuck him in, didn't you?''

''He's too old to be tucked in.''

Cheyenne swallowed her exasperation. Thomas's lack of parenting skills wasn't the issue now. They'd already wasted too much time on the telephone. ''I'll ask around here and find out if anyone has seen him. If not, I'll get dressed and head out on foot. He can't have gone far.'' She hesitated. ''We'll find him, Thomas. Davy's a smart kid. He'll be okay.''

''He won't be when I get through with him.''

Cheyenne winced at the crash on the other end of the line as Thomas hung up. She knew his anger came from worry over Davy.

Several hours later that worry had intensified. Davy had vanished into thin air. Nobody voiced their deepest fear.

Thomas put down the telephone receiver in the suite. ''Nothing. When I find that kid...'' He yanked at his loosened tie, and when it came off, looked at it as if he had no idea what it was. He tossed the tie in the direction of the nearest chair. ''Why the hell do we pay taxes if everyone is going to sit around on their behinds and do nothing? Giving me all that garbage about it being too early to call in the FBI.''

Cheyenne picked the tie up from the floor and draped it over the back of the chair. ''The police and the sheriff's office are searching. The state patrol has been notified. Worth has organized a search party of locals who know the area and have ideas where to look. Allie took Moonie to see if he could pick up Davy's scent. Mom's at our condo if Davy goes there. As much of the hotel staff as can be spared is out looking. We'll find him.''

''We should have found him by now. He's only seven.'' Staring at the ceiling, he ran his hands through increasingly disordered hair. ''C'mon, Thomas, think, think.''

Hearing the frustration and anguish in his voice, Cheyenne wanted to go to him. To give him comfort. Knowing he'd reject it, she stared at the pad in front of her. The penciled words wavered before her eyes.

"The gondola. He loved taking the gondola. He must have somehow got on it."

"Greeley checked, but she'll keep checking. The gondola operators have been notified."

"I can't stand around here waiting. I'm going to find him. Everyone has my cell phone number if—when they find him."

Cheyenne stood. "I'll go with you."

"Why? To make sure I don't beat him when I find him?"

"We can backtrack all the places Davy and I went to."

"Places I wouldn't know about because I didn't bother to go along? Places I wouldn't think of because I'm no good at taking care of a kid? I know what you're thinking. Satisfied, Ms. Lassiter? You had me pegged for a villain before we ever met. Does it feel good to be proved right?"

"Don't blame yourself, Thomas."

"I'm not blaming myself. This is your fault. You made the poor kid like you, and then you threw him away."

Stunned by Thomas's accusations, she couldn't say anything for a moment. "I didn't—"

"Little Miss Busybody. Sticking your nose in other people's business. Telling me how I should act, what I should do, and then, when your little experiment in behavior modification failed, you went your merry way, not giving a damn about the disaster you left in your wake."

Knowing what lay behind Thomas's hurtful words did little to deflect the pain. "I know you're worried about Davy," she said shakily. "I know—"

"Nothing. You could have prevented this, but you're too good to marry the likes of me and take care of my nephew." He wrenched open the door to his suite and threw his final words over his shoulder as he left. "No matter what kind of condition we find Davy in, I never want to see you again. Get out of my hotel. Get out of my life." The slam of the door reverberated through the room.

Cheyenne stood rooted to the floor. Waves of emotion buffeted her with the fury of a spring chinook. If Thomas had hurled stones at her, he couldn't have shocked her more. Or hurt her more. He sounded as if he hated her.

She'd meant well.

How lame that sounded.

The pad in her hand went flying across the room. Darn it, she was right. Thomas and Davy did belong together.

Thomas had asked her to marry him for all the wrong reasons and she'd refused him for all the right ones. If she'd agreed to his proposal, he could have lied to himself the rest of his life about his feelings for Davy.

Davy's running away had stripped away Thomas's protective layers. Never again could he say his nephew meant nothing to him.

Cheyenne felt the moisture on her cheeks. Davy had to be found. Thomas needed his nephew and now he knew it.

Being right was a wonderful thing. She wiped her cheeks with the back of her hand. The minute Davy showed up, she'd stick her face in Thomas's and tell him, "I told you so."

Except Thomas never wanted to see her again.

He hated her.

She'd never dreamed being right would be so painful. So lonely.

"We thought David was kidnapped once."

Cheyenne spun around at the voice behind her. "Davy hasn't been kidnapped. He just went somewhere for some reason."

"It goes with the territory," Ellen Steele said. "Disgruntled employees, or people see a big hotel and think the owners must be rich. I felt so helpless then, too, but with these excruciating headaches brought on by worry, I'd be in the way.''

"I didn't know Davy's father had been kidnapped.''

Thomas's mother gestured wearily. "It turned out David was being naughty. They found him curled up in the hotel basement with a filthy stray dog I'd forbidden him to keep. He insisted the dog was his friend.'' Her nose curled in distaste. "A mongrel.''

At Mrs. Steele's words, a fragment of memory danced elusively through Cheyenne's mind. Something Davy had said. She'd been reading him a book about a boy's dog, who always knew the boy's thoughts. Davy had asked if people and dogs understood each other, and when she'd said it seemed so to her, Davy had shyly confided he and Slots kind of talked to each other.

Mrs. Steele advanced into the room, expanding on the thankless aspects of parenthood.

Cheyenne looked at the older woman, blinked out of her trance and said, "Call Frank McCall and tell him I'm going to check the ranch again. I think that's where Davy is headed. Tell Frank to tell the others.'' Dashing out the door, she added, "I'll call if I find Davy.''

Hope Valley had never seemed so far away. Cheyenne wanted to ram the tourists as they crawled along Highway 82 admiring the scenery. Once off the highway, she slowed, searching for possible resting places for a seven-year-old boy.

They'd checked the ranch too early. It would have taken Davy a while to figure out how to get there. They'd questioned the R.F.T.A. bus drivers, but none remembered a small boy alone boarding a bus headed down valley, nor had anyone seen him trudging beside the highway.

As she crept along the dirt road, Cheyenne kept telling herself Davy had headed for the Double Nickel Ranch. Davy knew few people in Aspen and those few worked for the hotel. He wouldn't go to his uncle's employees, knowing they'd take him back to his uncle. She refused to consider that Davy might not have left of his own choice.

Why hadn't Davy come to her condo? Thomas claimed he hadn't said anything about her to Davy, but children sensed a lot more than most adults gave them credit for. Hearing something in Thomas's voice, Davy would have put his own interpretation on his uncle's words.

She gripped the steering wheel so hard her knuckles turned white. Davy could have sensed Thomas's anger and thought Cheyenne had terminated their arrangement. If Davy felt hurt, rejected and abandoned, he'd seek comfort from a friend who wouldn't scold him for running away. Who wouldn't call his uncle.

A pony friend named Slots.

At the ranch house, Cheyenne stood still and listened. Shadow, blind and deaf, dozed in a patch of sunlight ignoring the jay squawking from a cottonwood tree. A black and white barn cat shot from the barn. The horses penned in the nearest corral stood with their heads pointed toward the barn.

Her legs almost buckled with relief. Davy was in the barn.

Inside the huge building, an unnatural silence enveloped Cheyenne. Worth had turned the animals out, but there should be whispering birds, scurrying mice, rustling cats. An uneasy feeling crawled up her spine as she stood motionless, waiting for her eyes to adjust to the shadows.

"Been waiting for you, teach."

They sat on a hay bale halfway down the center of the barn. Davy and Harold Karper, the man who'd abused his stepson. The man whose wife had lost custody of her son. The man who blamed Cheyenne for all his troubles.

Thomas had never more wanted a place to live up to its name. Hope Valley. He saw Cheyenne's car immediately. She'd parked in a hurry, and the driver's door hung open.

Stepping from his borrowed car, Thomas heard a persistent beep. Cheyenne had left her keys in the ignition. He grabbed them and ran to the house.

Several minutes of yelling and searching convinced him Cheyenne and Davy were nowhere inside. Thomas stood on the front porch of the ranch house and searched the surroundings with his eyes. Behind the barn, almost hidden from the house and out of sight to anyone driving up, sat an unfamiliar pickup.

The hairs at the back of his neck prickled, and a sixth sense warned Thomas not to call out. Something was wrong.

Stepping back into the porch shadows, he made a call on his cellular phone. After a few seconds of whispered explanation, he listened a moment, then said, "I'm not waiting," and clicked off the phone in the middle of the speaker's response.

Making his way circuitously around the yard, Thomas kept an eye on the barn, especially on the opening high in the loft. No heads showed. Damned kid had no business taking off. As for Cheyenne haring after him... The two of them didn't have a brain between them. He'd wring both their necks.

At the corner of the barn he paused, listening. Voices came from inside. Unable to distinguish the words, Thomas edged toward the open barn door. A slit above the door hinges allowed him to see inside. The sight which greeted him froze his blood.

A strange man leaned his elbow against the door to an empty stall in the center of the barn. The man took a swig out of a whiskey bottle. With his other hand, he flicked on and off a cigarette lighter.

Thomas swore under his breath as he registered the implications of a cigarette lighter in a barn.

Behind the man, Davy sat tied to a post. Only his enormous eyes moved, flicking from the stranger to Cheyenne and back again. Seeing the fear on his nephew's face, Thomas had to fight the urge to rush recklessly into the barn.

Cheyenne stood with her back to Thomas, her legs apart, her hands in her back pockets. Her rigid spine made a lie of the casual pose.

Thomas strained to hear the conversation.

The man gave a high-pitched laugh. "Wrong, teach. Nobody's coming. I was snooping around the search party to see what all the excitement was about and I heard your brother say you'd gone to check the ranch. I started talk that someone saw a kid walking along Highway 82 heading up toward Independence Pass." He laughed again. "Like herding sheep. They all took off." He drank from the bottle. "It was easy to beat you here. You didn't even see me pass you on the road. The kid had taken the bus with some family, but he'd been walking since the highway. He was glad to get a lift to the ranch."

Cheyenne casually scuffed the dirt at her feet. "What do you want, Mr. Karper?"

The man's name rang a bell. Thomas searched his mind for where he'd heard it. The answer came quickly. The stepfather Cheyenne had told him about in New York. The man she'd reported for beating his stepson.

Karper unsteadily pointed his bottle at her. "You got me in a lot of trouble, teach. Lying to the police about me. Getting the brat to lie so the police took him away. Good riddance, I said, but my wife bawled about it so much, I had to give her something to bawl about." He took a swig from his bottle, then scowled at Cheyenne. "I just belted her a little, but she left. Only 'fore she left she gave some song and dance to my boss and I lost my job." He took another swig. "Your fault." Wiping his mouth on his shirt sleeve, he added, "You owe me."

Cheyenne shuffled her feet again. "This has nothing to

do with Davy. Let him go.'' Her calm voice quivered only once. On Davy's name.

Thomas saw red. He'd never before felt this savage desire to hurt someone. Moistening lips dried by fear, he moved sideways to lean against the side of the barn while he fought for control. Going off half-cocked would worsen an already dangerous situation. The man was a bomb about to explode.

Ruthlessly, Thomas thrust worries for Davy and Cheyenne from his brain. Think, Thomas, think. He quickly came up with a million rescue plans and just as quickly discarded them. Panic licked at his veins. He had to defuse the situation. Worth and the others wouldn't get here soon enough.

Swinging around, Thomas looked into the barn again.

The tableau remained unchanged. Thomas squinted. Something was different. Cheyenne had moved closer to Davy. Only a few inches, but she'd moved. The man tilted the bottle to his lips. Cheyenne took another step. She had one hand still in her pocket. The other hand rested on the back of her hip. Thomas concentrated on that hand. She was working a tiny pocketknife, trying to open it with one hand without dropping it.

The man pointed his bottle at Cheyenne and said in a slurred voice, ''You shouldn't of run off, honey. Now I'll have to punish you for being naughty.''

''I'm not your honey.'' Shuffling her feet, Cheyenne managed to close the distance between her and Davy another two inches.

''Don't back talk me. You know I don't like it when you back talk me.''

Thomas's stomach painfully convulsed. The man was drunk or crazy or both. He'd confused Cheyenne with his wife. Thomas wanted to scream at Cheyenne to keep her mouth shut. To avoid goading the man into action. Maybe his thoughts reached her. Miraculously, she said nothing.

"After I take care of you, I'll take care of your brat." Karper gave an insane giggle. "I told you when I married you, honey, I'd take care of him, didn't I?" He flicked on the lighter and grinned at the flame. "I like burning little boys. And their mamas."

Thomas almost lost it. Slamming a lid on his emotions, he concentrated on finding a way to neutralize Karper. The lighter scared Thomas. He didn't give a damn about the barn, but the distance between him and Davy was too great. He couldn't risk not reaching him in time. A risk he'd have to take if no other option presented itself. Beads of sweat covered his brow.

A horse neighed, and a plan popped into Thomas's mind. He'd run halfway to the house before he'd worked out the details. There weren't that many. Move horses into the barn to distract Karper, giving Cheyenne an opportunity to free Davy. Thomas would take care of the slimeball.

The plan worked better than he hoped. The big geldings, Payroll and Denver Mint, snorted and crowded suspiciously back against the rails, but Slots, Copper and Casino trotted eagerly toward the apples Thomas had grabbed from the refrigerator. Using the apples, he lured the horses to the barn, then rolled an apple through the open barn door. Slots eagerly followed the apple in. Thomas rolled in more apples. Copper and Casino crowded each other in their eagerness to get to the apples. A drumming of hooves and the two geldings joined those in the barn.

Shouted swearwords, sharp with fear, came from inside.

Thomas dashed around to the door at the other end of the barn. His fist met Karper on his way out. It wasn't Thomas's fault Karper made the mistake of trying to get up from the ground.

Worth and two law enforcement officers ran up as Thomas rubbed his right hand. Looking at the man lying in the dust at Thomas's feet, they listened to Thomas's short, precise explanation, then hauled Karper away.

"What's this?" Worth bent down.

Karper's lighter lay in the dirt at Thomas's feet. "Leave it. It's evidence."

A whirlwind flew from the barn and into Thomas's arms. "Uncle Thomas!"

Thomas wrapped his arms around Davy. Not that he needed to. His nephew clung to him tighter than a burr. "Do you have any idea how much trouble you've caused?" He hardly recognized the harsh croak as his own voice.

"Uncle Thomas, you're squeezing my middle out."

He laughed, light-headed with relief. "That's what happens when little boys run away. When they're found, people hug them until it hurts."

"It doesn't hurt," Davy said. "It feels good. Hey, Worth, look! Uncle Thomas and me decided we like hugging."

Thomas looked over Davy's head. "I'm sorry about the horses. I'll help you round them up."

"Don't worry about them," Worth said. "Allie's here. You better go up to the house and get that hand taken care of."

Thomas looked at his bleeding knuckles. They'd started to sting. "I will." He set Davy on the ground. "Go help Allie with the horses. You're the reason they're out."

Davy hung his head. "You mad at me?"

"Furious." As soon as body parts like his heart started operating properly again, Thomas would give Davy a sermon that set his hair on fire. Fire. He barely controlled a shudder.

"Going to beat me?"

"At what?" Thomas asked dryly. "Catching fish?"

Davy glanced up hopefully. "You're not mad?"

Thomas took a deep breath. Parenthood wouldn't be easy. He wanted to hug Davy until the boy's insides popped out. He wanted to break a brick over his head. He squatted down and looked his nephew in the eye. "I don't like what you did this morning. Running away and getting everyone upset was a bad thing to do. Worse, you put Cheyenne in danger." His stomach cramped. "I'm not going to beat you, but we have to talk about this later. Now, you go help round up those horses." Thomas stood. "Scoot."

Davy scooted.

"When you're ready, the law wants to talk to you and Davy," Worth said. "They've talked to Cheyenne." He nodded toward the barn. "She's in there."

She sat on the hay bale where Davy had been.

Thomas sat down beside her. "You okay?"

"Yes. Thank you. It was you who sent in the horses. I saw you hit Karper. How did you guess he was terrified of horses?"

"I didn't. I was trying to distract him." Cheyenne wouldn't look at him but he saw the damp tear tracks down her cheeks. He wanted to take her in his arms and hold her until her shuddering little breaths stopped and she breathed normally.

So he yelled at her. "What the hell were you doing, galloping out here like the Lone Ranger to the rescue?"

She jumped, her arm brushing against him. "How was I supposed to know that jerk was here? I expected to find Davy out at the corral talking to Slots."

"You should have waited for me."

"Why? You arrived in time to play hero."

"That is not the point," he said through locked teeth. She'd scared the hell out of him.

"It's exactly the point. It's my fault Davy was in danger. If I hadn't gone to the authorities about Michael's stepfather, if I hadn't tried to interfere in your relationship with Davy..." She tried to turn a shaky breath into a shrug. "I have the answer to everything. Except how to save a scared little boy."

A drop of blood fell to her jeans, joining a small, spreading stain. "Let me see your hand."

"No." She covered her clenched fist with her other hand.

Thomas grabbed her hand and forced open her fingers. She'd opened the tiny folded knife. Compressing his lips tightly, Thomas plucked the knife from her, pulled a white handkerchief from his pocket and pressed it against the red streak running down the center of her palm. "Did you do that trying to open the knife?" He curled her fingers over the hanky to hold the makeshift bandage in place.

She looked down at her hand. "No. I don't know. I must have done it after I cut Davy free."

"Go up to the house and clean it good."

"I will. In a minute. Don't worry about it."

The toneless voice sounded so unlike Cheyenne, Thomas gave her a second look, and cursed himself for not noticing the wide, staring eyes earlier. He put his arm around her. A wooden post had more give to it. "I'll wait until you're ready to go up."

"Why? You think I can't make it to the house by myself? You think I was so scared my legs won't hold me up? You think just because I failed to help Davy, I'm incapable of walking across the yard?"

Anger was better than apathy. Even if she was wrong. He'd kiss her if he wasn't so damned mad at her. "You didn't have to argue with Karper and antagonize him."

"Excuse me?" Outrage filled her voice.

She could be as outraged as she wanted. She hadn't been the one outside the barn feeling as helpless as a newborn baby. "And that waltzing around to get to Davy. A herd of rampaging elephants moves with more subtlety. It's a wonder Karper didn't beam you over the head with his damned whiskey bottle. Don't you ever stop and think before you leap into action?" He wouldn't have thought it possible for her to grow stiffer.

"Obviously not," she said in arctic tones. "I believe

you've already made your position clear on my interfering ways, so I don't know why you are hanging around here.'' She glared at the hand on her shoulder. ''If you're waiting for sympathy over your bleeding knuckles and for me to tell you what a big brave man you are, forget it. If you're waiting for gratitude, I thanked you once.''

''I'm not looking for gratitude.'' How had he ever thought he could marry her?

How could he not?

''Then what's keeping you? You don't ever want to see me again, remember? Maybe you can find a woman at Belly's who won't care about your sterile existence or your refusal to love. Let her fawn over you.''

To hell with the consequences. He had to kiss her.

The instant Thomas covered her lips with his, Cheyenne flung her arms around his middle and practically climbed into his mouth. He thought about telling her to slow down. He didn't think about it long. She plastered herself to his body, her palms pressing against his back. Thomas spared the tiniest part of a second to wonder if blood would come out of his silk-wool-blend suit coat, then decided he didn't give a damn.

He loved her hair. The bouncy curls wrapped about his fingers, tying her to him. The barn smells receded. He couldn't put a name to her scent. Except to call it Cheyenne.

He loved it.

He loved her blue shirt. He loved the way the warmth from her skin filtered through the thin fabric to heat every part of his body.

He loved the way her jeans hugged her bottom. The way he intended to hug her bottom. Without jeans.

He loved the hot, heavy feel of her breasts against his chest. He'd love them more when he'd removed her clothes.

He loved the enthusiastic way she kissed. The way her hands traveled around his body.

He loved how she'd ripped off his shirt in New York. A favor he intended to return.

He loved the way she clutched frantically at him when he shifted position. As if she was keeping him from leaving. He had no intention of leaving. Sliding to his knees, he pulled her down and then followed her to the floor.

He loved how her lips never left his.

He loved how her long legs fit between his thighs.

He loved the hot, tight, intense way she made him feel.

He slid his hands between them and took hold of the front edges of her shirt.

"I came to ask if you two are okay, but I think my question's been answered."

Tearing his mouth from Cheyenne's, Thomas looked up. Worth stood silhouetted in the large doorway. Allie and Greeley stood beside their brother, and Mary Lassiter stood on her son's other side, her arm around Davy.

Thomas braced his upper body on his hands and groped for something to say.

Davy detached himself from the group in the doorway and ran into the barn. "We got the horses put away. I put Slots in the corral all by myself," he added proudly. "Did you want to talk to me now?"

"Ah..." Hell, no, Thomas didn't want to talk to his nephew now. He wanted to make mad, passionate love in a barn. How the mighty have fallen, he thought ruefully.

"Davy," Mary said, "let's go up to the house and have something to eat. You must be starving and I don't think Worth ate all the chocolate cake I baked yesterday."

"I didn't? I better go help Davy get rid of it. What do you say, Davy? Race you to the cake."

"Just a minute," Thomas said. "Davy, before you eat, call your grandmother and apologize for the worry you caused her."

"Okay."

"One other thing." Thomas's first thought had been gratitude that Cheyenne's family hadn't shown up five minutes later. His second was that he had to somehow explain the scene they'd walked in on.

Her family waited.

He'd been rolling around on the barn floor with their sister and daughter.

They expected something from him.

Why wouldn't they? He hadn't even had the brains to remove himself from Cheyenne's body. She lay perfectly still beneath him. If her chest didn't push against him with each breath she took, he'd think a mannequin lay beneath him.

She'd said nothing.

No defensive words. No explanation.

Leaving him to do the talking.

It didn't take an Einstein to figure out why. She'd shown him her feelings.

A different kind of warmth filled him. Rolling carefully off Cheyenne, he stood, then reached down a hand to help her up. As soon as she gained her feet, he looked at the group in the doorway. "I hope you have more than a little chocolate cake, Mary, because we need something for a celebration. Cheyenne and I are going to be married."

Pandemonium broke out, Davy and all the Lassiters talking at once. Except for one Lassiter. Everyone's congratulations and questions died away as they belatedly perceived the look of furious disbelief on Cheyenne's face.

When she finally spoke, her voice shook with rage. "You are the most self-centered, selfish, egotistical man I've ever had the misfortune to meet. I told you I wouldn't marry you and I don't care if you're James Bond and Superman wrapped up in one, I haven't changed my mind. Did you really think I'd feel obligated to marry you just because you came to my rescue?"

Thomas opened his mouth but she didn't even stop to breathe.

"No, that wasn't it. You thought after I kissed you, if you announced to my family we were getting married, I'd be too embarrassed to deny it. Well, I'm not too embarrassed. You can't bully me and you can't blackmail me." She whirled to face the frozen onlookers. "I wouldn't marry him for all the Steele hotels and he knows it because I already told him so." She stomped out of the barn.

Thomas couldn't move, couldn't breathe, couldn't think. She had to marry him. How could she walk out on him? Leave him? How could he have been so wrong?

Hesitantly, Davy walked up to Thomas. "How come Cheyenne yelled at you?"

Thomas could tell her family was equally interested in the answer. He managed a shamefaced smile. "I guess I assumed a little too much. I thought things had changed. I should have asked her."

Worth shook his head. "Thomas, you have stepped in it big time."

He knew that. What he didn't know was what to do about it. "Davy, I'm sorry about the chocolate cake, but I think we better return to town. Cheyenne won't want me to stay."

Not one of the Lassiters disagreed with him.

CHAPTER TEN

"MARRIED!" Cheyenne marched the length of her living room, then whirled and shot daggers at Allie. "I can't believe he had the gall to say that. After I told him I absolutely would not marry him. And my own family, congratulating him. As if you believed him and actually approved."

"Considering the circumstances, his announcement seemed perfectly reasonable."

"Because you saw us kissing? We don't live in the Dark Ages anymore."

"Let it go, Cheyenne," Allie said wearily. "You've been ranting and raving since we came home yesterday. I didn't think you were ever going to let me go to sleep last night."

"He had no right. I told him no when he put his business proposal on the table the other morning. Where he got off telling my family…" She clenched her fists at her sides. "He's decided he wants me to raise Davy for him, and he thought his stupid announcement would force me into marrying him." A sneer contorted her face. "Nannies must come pretty dear these days. You'll never guess what he offered me if I'd marry him."

"Since you've told me several million times in the last hour alone, I don't need to guess."

"I can't believe, after I had carefully explained why I would not marry him, he'd turn around and tell everyone we were getting married. He didn't even bother to ask me again. And no—" Cheyenne turned on her sister "—that's not why I'm furious."

Cheyenne didn't blame Allie for not answering. They'd

been having this discussion, admittedly more of a monologue on her part, since yesterday. Every time she thought of Thomas Steele brazenly standing there in her family's barn saying they were getting married, she wanted to throw back her head and shriek. Break things. Break Thomas's head.

How could he do that to her?

So she'd kissed him. With enthusiasm. She didn't deny it. Anyone with more brains than ego—which certainly excluded Thomas Steele—would have realized her kisses were the aftermath of being scared half to death and had nothing at all to do with passion or even liking Thomas Steele.

Once she'd thought she'd fallen in love with him. She knew better now. Even she wasn't stupid enough to fall in love with an egotistical idiot.

Thomas had obviously thought so, announcing they were getting married.

If she never saw him again she'd be perfectly happy. Ecstatic.

"Do you want the last of this cereal?" Allie asked.

"I'm not hungry."

"You didn't eat dinner last night."

Cheyenne spun around and stared blindly out the window, hiding her face from Allie. How was she supposed to eat when her insides had been replaced with a huge, aching, black hole?

Maybe she had loved him. So what? It was yesterday's news.

If he'd cared for her the tiniest little bit, he wouldn't have treated her so shabbily. He cared about nothing beyond his own selfish need to find someone to care for Davy.

Cheyenne ignored the ringing phone.

It wouldn't be Thomas. After she'd walked out of the barn, he hadn't followed her. Hadn't bothered to try and convince her he loved her. Not that he could convince her. She knew exactly how he felt about her.

The lump in her throat grew painfully large. Allie was right. She had to quit thinking about it. About him.

She'd concentrate on business. Allie could take the day off. Cheyenne turned to her sister.

Allie was on the phone. "Quit laughing, Worth," she said, laughing herself, "I can't understand you. What? Yes, the paper's here. No, we haven't read... What? Quit laughing. You're kidding? What page?" She listened a minute. "Sure, sacrifice me," Allie said and hung up the phone.

"What was that all about?"

"Worth being Worth. Where's that page?" Allie muttered to herself, leafing furiously through the newspaper. She stopped turning pages, held up the paper and started reading. Chuckles came from behind the paper.

"What?"

"Just a minute." Allie moved the paper out of Cheyenne's reach. "Let me finish, then you can have—" A choke of laughter cut off her words.

Cheyenne tried to read over Allie's shoulder, but her sister bumped her away. "Wait your turn."

"You're reading the Want Ads. What can be so funny about them?"

Allie laid down the newspaper. "Start at the top left," she said, "and keep going."

Cheyenne read the first Want Ad. Blinked and read it again in disbelief.

Want wife. Has to like little boys, tall buildings, kissing on barn floors, fishing, horseback riding and hopeless men. Room 301, The St. Christopher Hotel, Aspen.

The next ad read:

Want wife. Has to have sport-utility vehicle, dangerous pocketknife, long legs and huge heart. Room 301, The St. Christopher Hotel, Aspen.

The ads continued down the page and spilled over to the next column. And the next and the next. Cheyenne gave Allie a horrified look and kept reading. Each ad was different.

Each ridiculed Cheyenne. This was Thomas Steele's idea of revenge.

She was going to kill him.

"I can't decide which is my favorite," Allie said, "this one or this one." She pointed out two ads in the last column.

Cheyenne hadn't read that far. She read them now.

Want wife. Has to have frizzy blond—not bleached— hair and muddy blue eyes. Room 301, the St. Christopher Hotel, Aspen.

Want wife. Has to be busybody with answer for everything. Make my answer yes. Room 301, the St. Christopher Hotel, Aspen.

Cheyenne quit reading. She grabbed the newspaper and headed for the front door.

"You might want to change your clothes first," Allie called.

Looking down at her pajamas, Cheyenne skidded to a halt. She couldn't rip him apart from head to toe wearing pajamas.

Minutes later, dressed for battle in blue jeans and a black sweatshirt, she marched through the streets of Aspen. She hadn't gone ten feet before it became apparent the entire population of town had read the newspaper and knew who was Thomas Steele's target. Red flags of mortification waved on her cheeks as she passed friends and neighbors, all of whom could barely control their amusement.

Thomas Steele was going to pay.

Maybe she had interfered. Maybe she should have minded her own business. Not the first time. Nobody could fault her for checking on the well-being of a child. But once she'd satisfied herself Davy wasn't abused, she didn't have to stick around and try and mold Thomas and Davy into a family unit. She'd been so certain she knew all the answers.

She knew she'd interfered for Davy's sake.

Had she?

Or because she'd been attracted to Thomas?

Which proved she was an idiot. Attracted to an egotistical male who hated her so much, he'd plastered his ill will all over the newspaper.

She stoked her anger. Anger left no room for hurt. And betrayal. She could accept he couldn't love her. Eventually. The pain came in acknowledging he didn't even want friendship from her. She dashed away a tear. She didn't want friendship from a jerk like him. She wouldn't cry.

Not now.

She'd barely beat once on the door to his suite before Thomas flung open the door and hauled her inside.

"Where the hell have you been? Davy, go tell McCall if he puts through one more phone call, unless it's from a Lassiter, I'll rip out the phone lines."

"Okay." Davy beamed at Cheyenne. "We're gonna have champagne and strawberries."

"Go." Thomas pointed to the door.

"Okay." Davy continued to beam at Cheyenne. "I wanted to put in about baking cookies, but Uncle Thomas said as long as we can eat your mom's chocolate cake, it don't matter if you can bake cookies."

"Out!"

"Okay." Davy stopped in the middle of closing the door and grinned at Cheyenne. "I'll be back."

Cheyenne gaped at the closed door as the ramifications of Davy's behavior sank in. She'd been wrong about

Thomas's motivation in placing the ads. The ads weren't about revenge. Thomas was still trying to force her into marrying him so she could take care of Davy. Totally ignoring her feelings, Thomas had increased the pressure on her. He didn't think she could turn him down in front of the entire town. Even worse, he'd enlisted Davy. If by some chance, she didn't care that she was the laughingstock of Aspen, then she wouldn't turn him down for fear of breaking a little boy's heart.

As she worked out Thomas's diabolical scheme, the rate at which she batted her leg with the rolled-up newspaper increased a thousand percent. "I'm not going to marry you," she said through clenched teeth, "and I want an apology—in print—for that garbage you put in the paper today."

"What took you so long to read the paper and get over here? People born on a ranch are supposed to get up with the sun. Do you have any idea how many women have answered those ads? The phone started ringing at six-thirty, and there's been a parade of women claiming to have frizzy hair and muddy blue eyes. Most of them are tourists. What are tourists doing reading the Want Ads in the newspaper? They're on vacation."

She couldn't believe the outrage in his voice. How dare he be outraged! She swung the newspaper at him.

Thomas ducked, grabbed the paper and tossed it across the room. "Wait a minute. Are you mad at me?"

All power of speech failed her. She could only stare at him.

"I'm sorry. The morning hasn't gone quite as I planned." He gestured at himself. "I haven't shaved, and I know how you feel about knobby knees. I can't do anything about the knees."

His hair stood up in tufts, he wore the silk bathrobe, and stubble on his face made him look twice as sexy. She didn't trust the smile on his face. Thomas Steele didn't have tentative smiles. He didn't know the meaning of the word uncertain. He couldn't possibly be as confused as she was.

Cheyenne backed toward the door. "I came to tell you I want a retraction." How did one retract a Want Ad? "Or whatever."

"I vote for whatever." Thomas beat her to the door and stood in front of it, a solid barrier between her and escape. "Such as you marrying me."

Quick tears sprang to her eyes. "Let it go. I said no."

"Say yes." He wiped a tear from her cheek with his thumb. "Don't cry. It tears up my insides when you cry. Yesterday—" He cleared his throat. "After yesterday, I think I can deal with about anything. Except you not marrying me."

"Thomas, don't..."

"I thought I could walk away from Davy. Yesterday I knew I was lying to myself. I can't walk away from him. Davy and I need each other."

She'd longed for him to say those very words.

They cut painfully deep. Why couldn't he need her?

The way she needed him.

He had the most beautiful throat. And chest. His silk robe slid partially open. She wanted to burrow into his warm body.

"We need you."

She shook her head without looking up. If she looked up, she'd kiss him. If she kissed him... She loved his bony knees. "You can take care of Davy without me."

"I know that."

The simple admission brought her head sharply up. Her breath caught at the look in his eyes. She shook her head slowly. She must be wrong.

"Stop saying no, and listen." Thomas captured her face and held it immobile between his hands. His eyes blazed down at her. "Whatever happens to us, Davy is moving in with me. What's between you and me has nothing to do with Davy."

"Physical attraction," Cheyenne croaked.

"Hell, yes. It's all I can do not to tear your clothes off right now, but… Damn it, I've been practicing all morning. Let me get the words out."

She didn't want to hear. She couldn't bear it if she was wrong.

His hands pressed against her cheeks, he wouldn't let her shake her head. "Listen, damn it. I thought I could walk away from you. I was a fool, an idiot, call me whatever name you want, you can't call me worse than I've called myself. You were right. I am stupid."

She couldn't have moved if he'd let her. Or taken her eyes from his face. A face which spoke more than words. Hope began filling her heart.

"You have no idea how much I need you. I want to walk into a room and have you welcome me into your arms, the way you welcome Davy. I want to hear your laughter. I want to wake up with your hair tickling my nose. I want you to care about me, to tell me when I'm wrong, approve when I'm right. I want you to bear my children and rock them in my grandmother's rocking chair. I want to tell you about my life. I want to know every detail of yours. I want to know your favorite foods, your favorite movies. I want you in my life. I want in your life. I need you."

Cheyenne burst into tears.

Thomas dropped his hands. "I'm sorry." He stepped around her and walked away. "I know you said you didn't want to marry me. I thought, I hoped, if you knew I wanted to marry you for reasons other than to be Davy's mother, it might make a difference to you. I won't bother you again. I'll put something in the paper tomorrow. I don't know what. I'll think of something."

Cheyenne turned. He stood at the window with his back

to her, his head bowed, his hands braced against the windowsill. She wiped her cheeks and sniffed. "From the back, your knees aren't that bad."

He slowly straightened. "What?"

Pulling a tissue from her pocket, she blew hard. "I could probably get used to them if the contract is right."

"Contract?" he repeated in a carefully neutral voice.

"The one covering all the eventualities. The assets you're offering me."

"Are you saying you'll marry me if we have a contract?"

Cheyenne almost laughed at his incredulous tone of voice. "You haven't asked me yet."

He turned slowly. "Cheyenne Lassiter, will you marry me? Will you be my wife for richer and poorer and all that stuff? Will you love me?"

"How could I turn down all those hotel suites?"

He didn't move. "Yes or no, damn it!"

"Yes."

He closed the distance between them. Some minutes later, Cheyenne drew back. Not that she wanted to stop kissing him. She never wanted to stop kissing him, but she'd remembered Davy's words. "Davy," she muttered, slapping Thomas's hands aside and pulling down her sweatshirt.

"Let him find his own girl."

"He said he'd be back."

"Uh-huh." Thomas lifted her sweatshirt again and lowered his head.

The man had a one-track mind about everything. "Thomas." She repeated his name louder.

"What?"

"I love you."

"Good."

"You're supposed to say you love me."

"Uh-huh."

"Uh-huh, what? Uh-huh, you know you're supposed to, or uh-huh, you love me?"

"The latter."

She couldn't help laughing. "I guess Rome wasn't built in a day."

He lifted his head and straightened her sweatshirt. "I love the way you laugh. Your wrinkled eyes. I love your teeth."

"I am not even going to ask."

He grinned. "I better get dressed before everyone gets here."

Cheyenne froze. "Everyone gets here?"

"Didn't you hear Davy? Champagne and strawberries. Your family should be here by now. Don't give me that killing look. You already said yes. You can't back out now."

She would not respond to that loving smile on his face. If she let him manipulate her now... She folded her arms across her chest. "I haven't signed anything. Like a contract."

"Will you quit with the contract? It was stupid. I was stupid. There is not going to be any damned contract."

"I'm not getting married without a contract."

Her words wiped the remaining remnants of a grin off his face. "I refuse to believe you want a contract. You know everything I have will be yours."

She tapped her foot. "I want a contract."

"Hell." He strode over to the armoire and grabbed a pad and pencil. "All right. Tell me what the hell you want and we'll sign it right now." He slammed the pad on the table and sat. "Tell me. Name it. Whatever you want."

"Number one. From now on, I select your ties."

"What?"

She pointed to the pad. "Write it down." She waited until he'd finished. "Number two. You have to say I love you, the words—I love you—by our twenty-fifth anniversary. Write it down. Now sign it.''

He hesitated, then signed his name. Carefully he placed the pen beside the pad, lining the two up with exact precision. ''Will it bother you until I say it?'' he asked without looking up.

''No. If I can live with your bony knees, I can live with anything.''

Pulling her down on his lap, he brushed aside her hair and framed her face with his hands. ''I love your frizzy hair and I love your muddy blue eyes. I love the way you care about other people. I love the way you try and do what's right.''

She smoothed a tuft of hair. ''I love you, too.''

''Wait. I'm not done.'' He took a big breath. ''Cheyenne Lassiter, I love you. I love you more than I love the Steele hotels.''

Eventually she had to quit kissing him and come up for air. ''As much as I love you in that bathrobe, Thomas, you aren't going to be in it much longer if you don't quit kissing me like that.''

He gave her a sexy smile. ''I don't mind.''

''Davy and my family might.''

''Damn. Me and my great idea of a champagne celebration.'' He lifted her from his lap, stood, then set her on the chair. ''Don't go away while I get dressed.'' Through the open bedroom door, he yelled, ''I love you, soon-to-be Mrs. Steele.''

She knew she had a sappy grin on her face. She didn't care. The notepad caught her eye, and an irresistible urge to tease him seized her. ''I think turquoise with fuchsia and orange stripes will be perfect.''

Knotting a burgundy-colored tie, Thomas stuck his head through the door. ''What are you talking about?''

''The tie I'm going to buy you to wear for our wedding.''

His fingers froze. From across the room she watched him swallow.

He opened his mouth, shut it, opened it and tried once more. "If that's what you want me to wear," he swallowed again, "then it's perfect."

Her man of steel. With a loving heart.

EPILOGUE

THOMAS tipped the bellman, shut and locked the door to the suite at St. Chris's, then swung Cheyenne up into his arms. He loved the way she threw back her head and laughed. He loved everything about her, from her curly blond hair to the pink toenails peeking from her sandals. "Welcome home, Mrs. Steele."

She laughed again. "You're going to throw out your back if you don't quit carrying me across the threshold of our room in every Steele hotel we visit."

Besides the one in St. Bart's, which he hadn't even signed the papers on, he'd carried her across thresholds in New Orleans and Charleston. Now he smiled down at her. "I love carrying you. When I run out of thresholds, I'll buy more hotels."

Cheyenne laid her head on his shoulder. "Have I told you how much I love you?"

He pushed open the door to the bedroom. "Not in the last ten minutes. Tell me again." She looked fresh and cool in her silky, flowery dress. Thomas could hardly wait to remove it. Lying her on the bed, he bent over her, one hand resting on her warm thigh as she smiled up at him. Love spilled from her eyes. He still had trouble believing this incredible woman loved him. "It's been a long day of travel. I think we ought to rest up before we meet everyone for dinner."

Reaching for the ends of his iridescent teal silk tie, she pulled him down to her side. "We should call the ranch and tell Davy we're back."

Thomas unbuckled her sandals and threw them on the

floor beside his shoes. "You're probably right." He slid her dress inch by inch up her leg.

Cheyenne tossed his unknotted tie on the floor. "I know I'm right." She started on his buttons.

His shirt joined the tie and he unzipped her dress. "When I called from Charleston, I told Davy we'd see him at dinner." He slipped the dress down over her shoulders to her waist and pressed a kiss against her warm, silken back.

She made a sound deep in her throat and reached for his belt. "He's probably helping Worth shovel out the barn and won't want to be bothered."

"I wouldn't want to take him away from his favorite activity." Propping his upper body on an elbow, Thomas ran his other hand through the fragrant hair cascading over the pillow. His entire body tightened in anticipation.

Her eyes danced with laughter. "You mean you don't want to be taken away from your favorite activity."

"That, too," he agreed. If he'd wanted her before, he craved her now, this kind, generous, beautiful, exciting, stubborn, exasperating, meddlesome woman.

He wouldn't change a thing about her. His wife. His life's companion.

Cheyenne lay on her back, her eyes closed. The September sun found its way between the window's metal mullions to warm her bare breasts and legs. Her crumpled dress ringed her waist. They'd been too impatient to love each other to remove it. Cheyenne didn't have the energy now.

She didn't have the energy to phone Allie, either. Guilt stole over her. She should have called her sister the minute they arrived.

The breathing at her side changed and a warm hand slid across her stomach. "You're worrying about Allie again."

Opening her eyes, Cheyenne turned her head to scowl at Thomas. "It's creepy the way you read my mind."

Smiling, he pulled her skirt down over her legs. "Not your mind. Your face."

"Well, stop it." After a minute she added crossly, "You might as well go ahead and say it. We both know it's my fault. If I hadn't had the stupid idea of inviting Zane Peters to our wedding, Allie wouldn't be in this awful situation."

"Wait until you talk to Allie before you decide whether it's awful. Maybe they discovered they still love each other." He trailed his fingers across her bare chest.

Cheyenne refused to be diverted. "I told you what Greeley said. Allie wore blue jeans. Blue jeans! That doesn't sound like love to me."

"Listen up, Mrs. Steele." Thomas leaned over and grasped her chin, giving it a gentle shake. "Yes, you invited this Peters to our wedding, but Allie got herself into this situation, and if she wants out, she's perfectly capable of handling things on her own. You, Mrs. Steele, are to mind your own business."

She gave her dictator of a husband a smoldering look. "I have no intention of interfering in Allie's business," she said haughtily, ignoring the fact that as soon as she'd heard about Allie, Cheyenne had persuaded Thomas to cut their honeymoon short to rush back to Aspen.

"Liar," Thomas said in a loving voice. "Just remember you have a husband and a son to take care of now."

Cheyenne couldn't help smiling. "A son." Knowing how important having a mom could be to a child, she'd told Davy his mother would always be his mother, but he could call Cheyenne "Mom" if he wanted. That he wanted to filled her with joy.

Shifting so she half lay on Thomas, she hugged his middle. "I'm glad you decided you'd like Davy to call you Dad. He's going to be in seventh heaven."

"Dad." Thomas wore a silly grin on his face. "It has a good sound, doesn't it?" The grin slipped. "Davy might not think so."

That Thomas could show such unexpected vulnerability endeared him to Cheyenne. Foolish man. He'd make Davy and their babies a wonderful father. "If Davy doesn't want you as his dad, refuse to let him play with your train," she teased.

"How many times do I have to tell you, I bought the train for Davy?"

"I love you when you get all huffy and defensive." Her mouth closed over his nipple.

Thomas inhaled sharply. "I don't get huffy and defensive," he said in a ragged voice.

She walked her fingers down his stomach, thrilling at her power as his muscles tightened and clenched at her touch. His gold watch winked as a ray of sunlight hit it. "How long until dinner?"

Warm hands cradled her hips. "Long enough."

* * * * *

Look for Allie Lassiter's story.
Coming soon from
Jeanne Allan.

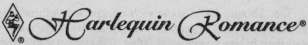

Harlequin Romance®

brings you four very special weddings to remember in our new series:

WHITE WEDDINGS

True love is worth waiting for....

Look out for the following titles by some of
your favorite authors:

August 1999—SHOTGUN BRIDEGROOM #3564
Day Leclaire
Everyone is determined to protect Annie's good name and ensure
that bad boy Sam's seduction attempts don't end in the
bedroom—but begin with a wedding!

September 1999—A WEDDING WORTH WAITING FOR #3569
Jessica Steele
Karrie was smitten by boss Farne Maitland. But she was
determined to be a virgin bride. There was only one solution:
marry and quickly!

October 1999—MARRYING MR. RIGHT #3573
Carolyn Greene
Greg was wrongly arrested on his wedding night for something he
didn't do! Now he's about to reclaim his virgin bride when he dis-
covers Christina's intention to marry someone else....

November 1999—AN INNOCENT BRIDE #3577
Betty Neels
Katrina didn't know it yet but Simon Glenville, the wonderful doctor
who'd cared for her sick aunt, was in love with her. When the time
was right, he was going to propose....

Available wherever Harlequin books are sold.

HARLEQUIN®

Makes any time special.™

HRWW

 **HARLEQUIN®**
Makes any time special ™

WIN A DREAM

In celebration of Harlequin®'s golden anniversary

Enter to win a *dream!* You could win:

- A luxurious trip for two to *The Renaissance Cottonwoods Resort* in Scottsdale, Arizona, or

- A bouquet of flowers once a week for a year from **FTD**, or

- A $500 shopping spree, or

- A fabulous bath & body gift basket, including **K-tel's** *Candlelight and Romance* 5-CD set.

Look for **WIN A DREAM** flash on specially marked Harlequin® titles by Penny Jordan, Dallas Schulze, Anne Stuart and Kristine Rolofson in October 1999*.

FTD

**RENAISSANCE.
COTTONWOODS RESORT**
SCOTTSDALE, ARIZONA

K-TEL

*No purchase necessary—for contest details send a self-addressed envelope to Harlequin Makes Any Time Special Contest, P.O. Box 9069, Buffalo, NY, 14269-9069 (include contest name on self-addressed envelope). Contest ends December 31, 1999. Open to U.S. and Canadian residents who are 18 or over. Void where prohibited.

PHMATS-GR

Coming Next Month

#3571 CLAIMING HIS CHILD Margaret Way
Nick and Suzannah had been deeply in love—until her father had forced him to leave town. Now he was back, unable to forgive Suzannah for marrying another man and having his child. But there was something about Suzannah's little girl that inexplicably drew Nick to her side....

#3572 DESERT HONEYMOON Anne Weale (author's 75th book!)
Clare knew Dr. Alexander Strathallen had vowed never to love again, but she couldn't resist his offer of a marriage of convenience. He only wanted her because she had a son and he needed an heir, but in the heat of the desert, maybe he'd realize he needed a wife, too!

#3573 MARRYING MR. RIGHT Carolyn Greene
Greg last saw Christina on their wedding night, when he was arrested for something that he didn't do. He'd always planned to prove himself worthy of Christina before returning to reclaim her as his virgin bride—and now he's back....

White Weddings: *True love is worth waiting for...*

#3574 THE TYCOON'S BABY Leigh Michaels
Single father Webb Copeland had no desire to remarry so he hired a pretend fiancée to keep his matchmaking grandmother at bay. Only, no sooner did Janey have his ring on her finger and his baby daughter in her arms than Webb wished it wasn't just a temporary arrangement!

Daddy Boom: *Who says bachelors and babies don't mix?*